# MEN
## *in* UNIFORM

Courteous, courageous and commanding—
these heroes lay it all on the line for the
people they love in more than fifty stories about
loyalty, bravery and romance.
Don't miss a single one!

# CAROLINE BURNES

## BABE IN THE WOODS

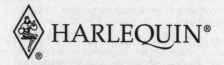

TORONTO • NEW YORK • LONDON
AMSTERDAM • PARIS • SYDNEY • HAMBURG
STOCKHOLM • ATHENS • TOKYO • MILAN • MADRID
PRAGUE • WARSAW • BUDAPEST • AUCKLAND

Recycling programs
for this product may
not exist in your area.

ISBN-13: 978-0-373-36279-0

BABE IN THE WOODS

**Printed in U.S.A.**

**CAROLINE BURNES**

continues her life as doorman and can opener for her six cats and three dogs. E. A. Poe, the prototype cat for her Fear Familiar series, rules as king of the ranch, followed by his lieutenants, Miss Vesta, Gumbo, Chester, Maggie the Cat and Ash. The dogs, though a more lowly life form, are tolerated as foot soldiers by the cats. They are Sweetie Pie, Maybelline and Corky.

To the staff of TLC,
who treat their human patients with as much tenderness
as their four-legged ones. And to Corky—irreplaceable.

# CHAPTER ONE

REBECCA BARRETT leaned into the whipping black mane of the stallion and gave him more rein. His pace increased, his huge hooves pounding as he raced through the dense green of an unfamiliar stretch of forest. She glanced behind her, her blood racing and her imagination running as wild as the horse. She couldn't see them, but she could hear the hooves pounding after her. The men rode spectacular horses, but none were a match for hers. Yet they were gaining on her—the forces of evil. She alone could deliver the single message that would save the world, and her only route to safety was to ride so fast they couldn't catch her.

A small tree had fallen over the middle of the woodland road. Rebecca suspected an ambush. Lifting out of the saddle only an inch, she felt the powerful muscles bunch beneath her, and then the horse curve under her as he sailed over the tree.

The exhilaration was almost more than she could stand. Diable was the finest horse she'd ever ridden, and she'd had more than her share of top-dollar rides. As a teenager in Tennessee, she'd been on the A Circuit. But this wasn't a horse for the show ring. This was a horse for adventure. This was Lightning, Fury, Trigger, Silver and the Black Stallion all rolled into one.

It was still spring in Mississippi, but the temperature was in the eighties and after a few more miles, she let Diable settle into a ground-covering trot. The exciting ride had been a terrific fantasy, but the only thing chasing her was new job duties. She had a million things to do, but one of the things she'd promised Aurelia and Marcus McNeese was that she'd exercise Diable, Cogar and Mariah. Who could ever imagine she'd find the job of her dreams that also included three wonderful horses? Fate had certainly smiled down on her when she'd applied to Blackthorn to oversee the renovation of the estate and the work on excavating an old Indian burial mound that looked as though it might become the richest source of information yet discovered into the lives of the Mound Builders.

As she and the horse drew closer to the burial mound, she slowed her pace. By the time she walked Diable from the mound to his barn, he'd be thoroughly cooled. She grinned at the thought of the barn—a magnificent structure, with an apartment for Joey Reynolds. The barn had been the first thing Marcus and Aurelia McNeese had built in their dream of making Blackthorn their home. The caretaker's cottage was where Rebecca called home while she worked at the estate. The newlyweds had big plans, and they'd hired Rebecca to make sure their plans were properly implemented while they took a long honeymoon in Europe. Rebecca had been left in charge of building, excavation and all other aspects of Blackthorn, including keeping an eye on Joey.

Rebecca reflected that the apartment for Joey was one of the biggest acts of kindness she'd ever heard of. And she'd never seen anyone love a place more than Joey loved Blackthorn. She could see him right now, weeding what had once been a formal garden. His back was soaked with sweat and the smile on his face seemed permanent. By the end of the summer, he'd have the garden back, blooming with lush beauty. Joey had a green thumb and infinite patience. He'd also put in a small vegetable patch that seemed to grow four inches every night. Rebecca teased him that he'd gotten the seeds from a magician and soon a beanstalk would be up in the clouds.

As enjoyable as Joey was, other aspects of the job were drawbacks, and the primary one was walking right toward her. "Get down off the horse. I want to talk to you."

Rebecca had long grown accustomed to Brett Gibson's imperious manner. She'd intended to dismount, so she did.

"I hope you've explained to that simpleton that he can't just start digging up the ground and planting things wherever he'd like," Brett said, using a glove to wipe the sweat from his eyes. "He's started a compost heap. He's wheeling barrows full of horse manure from the barn. I want him stopped right now."

Rebecca glanced over to the area Brett had indicated and saw that Joey, was, indeed, making a compost heap and not all that far from the burial mound. In her opinion, it was located far enough from where Brett was excavating the mound that it wouldn't bother him. It *shouldn't,* but it did. But what really troubled Brett was the fact that she and Joey were on Blackthorn soil at all.

"Joey talked over all his plans with Marcus and Aurelia before they left for Spain. I'm sure he wouldn't do anything they hadn't given approval for." She saw the anger flare in Brett's eyes. He hated the fact that she was his superior on this job. At times, it seemed he hated her. "And please don't call Joey a simpleton or any other names. He's a kind and gentle man and something like that would really hurt him."

"I didn't come here to baby-sit 'kind and gentle' people. I came here to do what may prove to be the most important excavation in this region."

"I understand the importance of your work, Brett. I'm trained in your field, though I chose the business side of it. But Joey's work is just as important to him as yours is to you."

"A garden isn't of any significance to anyone."

She could see the deep anger in Brett's gray eyes. He was red in the face and a vein was pulsing at his temple. A bit more of that in the hot sun and he'd have a stroke.

"Why don't you get a glass of water and take a break in the shade?"

"Don't patronize me," Brett said. His fingers closed on her arm as she started to turn away, but when he saw the look in her blue eyes, he released his grip. "I'm sorry. I didn't mean to grab you."

"I don't want anything untoward to happen while the McNeeses are away," Rebecca said. "We both know they left me in charge of everything that goes on at Blackthorn—including the new construction and the archaeological dig. I know you don't like it, but there it is. And I'm telling you to get a glass of water and find some shade."

She didn't wait for an argument. She led Diable away from Brett and the mound and toward the narrow trail that looped back to the stables. Her blue eyes were flashing with anger, but her breathing was calm and regular. Brett really aggravated her. He was a jackass. If Marcus and Aurelia had any idea of how he behaved toward Joey, they'd fire him.

Rebecca knew she could track them down in Spain, but she had no intention of disturbing their long-postponed honeymoon with squabbles between employees. She was in charge, and she'd handle it.

She swung back into the saddle and continued to the barn. She had to cut through a stretch of woods, and she welcomed the cool shade. Dang, it was so hot already. Only May and the promise of true summer made her doubt her toughness. She'd grown up in Memphis, but she'd spent the last ten years away. First on a scholarship at UCLA and then later in San Francisco where she quickly rose to the top of a real estate management firm and became the resident expert on historical architecture. That interest had driven her to study more design.

That, coupled with her business background, made her perfect for the job at Blackthorn.

A flit of movement caught her attention. Someone was in the woods with her. She felt a pinprick of concern. There'd been a murder in Blackthorn woods only a few months before. A woman had been killed. Aurelia had told her all about it—and about how Aurelia had been tried and found innocent of the murder.

Rebecca had been told to call the sheriff if there was any sign of meddling on the property. The intruder was hurrying along, unaware that she'd entered this part of the woods and had seen him.

"Hey!" she called out.

The man began to run.

"Hey! Come back here!" Rebecca gave chase. Diable was certainly faster than the man, but the woods were so thick the horse couldn't get into them.

She saw the bushes quake and quiver, the new green leaves marking the passage of the intruder as he headed toward the highway.

"This is private property. No trespassing allowed," she yelled after him.

It was probably some teenager, curious about what was going on at Blackthorn. Aurelia and Marcus had found the treasure that had been a source of hunts for decades. But some folks would only take that as encouragement that there was more treasure buried. Aurelia shook her head. Treasure hunts and casinos were two places it had never crossed her mind to believe she might get money.

She dismounted at the stables, unsaddled Diable, gave him a good rubdown and promised Cogar that he was next on the agenda for a ride.

When she got back to Blackthorn she went to the caretaker's cottage where she was bunking. She dialed the sheriff's office and dutifully reported the intruder. Rebecca was always good for her word.

SHERIFF DRU COLSON noted the overturned leaves. Someone had been in the woods at Blackthorn. Most likely just a curiosity seeker as Rebecca thought. Far more interesting than the disturbed leaves was the woman who'd reported them. He'd never seen eyes bluer than hers.

"Did you get a look at the intruder?" Dru asked as he rose to his feet. Rebecca Barrett was about five-six with honey-colored hair and a figure that did justice to the riding breeches and boots she wore.

"He was tall, a little on the thin side, sandy-colored hair. He was wearing some kind of plaid shirt, predominantly blue, and jeans."

Dru raised his eyebrows. She was also pretty cool in a situation. Few people noticed so many details.

"Did he say anything?"

She shook her head. "As soon as I called out to him, he took off running."

"I'm not happy with the fact that someone was out here. Most of the locals know the treasure is gone and after Lottie Levert's death, Blackthorn is off-limits."

"It was probably a kid." Rebecca nodded at that assessment. "He ran off like a sprinter."

"I'll call the principal at the high school and get him to make an announcement to the students, reminding them that trespassing is a criminal offense. Kids don't understand that any kind of trouble with the law has unforeseen repercussions."

"Thanks," Rebecca said. Her smile was warm, like sunshine.

"I knew the McNeeses had hired a crew up here, but I haven't seen the changes. Would you mind giving me a tour?"

"I'd love to. Shall we start with the barn? They've framed in the house, but it's a long way from show time."

Together they walked through the filtered sunlight of the woods. Dru felt the tension leaving his shoulders. He was reminded of being a boy, those golden days of total freedom and innocence when he'd played with his school friends. They'd had endless adventures playing Robin Hood or war or Tarzan, some of them in the woods of Blackthorn.

"It is beautiful here," Rebecca said, pointing to a cluster of wild orchids that were nestled in some pine needles.

"Blackthorn is one of the prettiest places on earth. I'm glad the McNeeses found the money so they can preserve the estate. How is work going on the main house?"

"Without a hitch," Rebecca said. "It's going to be a magnificent house. The plans are phenomenal."

"Batson and Batson are the architect and contractor, right?"

"Yes. Regina Batson is here on the job." She gave a crooked smile. "She came here to work with her parents, but I'm afraid her heart's been captured by the thrill of archaeology."

"Ah, the allure of the past. Still, it can't hurt to have the boss's daughter on-site. Batson and Batson stand behind their work. You shouldn't have any problems."

"That makes me feel better."

Dru grinned. He liked the idea that he made her feel better. She certainly made him feel alive. He caught a glimpse of the new barn through the trees and let out a low whistle. "Marcus loves those horses."

"Aurelia seems fond of them, too," Rebecca pointed out. "Especially Mariah. She loves that mare. Who wouldn't?"

"I've had a lot of training in the field of observation. You're a horsewoman, too, aren't you?"

Rebecca's laughter was full and free. "Very good, officer. You caught me with my boots on."

He felt a foolish grin touch his face and he didn't care. He was acting like a high-school boy when the prettiest girl in school had time to talk to him. It was fun.

"Never underestimate the value of good training."

She laughed again, and her hand brushed his arm. "I didn't realize you were a comedian. Aurelia never mentioned a word about it."

"I'm afraid Aurelia had a lot on her mind when we met. I never believed she was guilty of murdering Lottie Levert, but I had to charge her. All the evidence pointed to her."

"She told me, and she never bore any grudge against you."

"She's a terrific woman. I'm telling you, when she came into Natchez as the heiress of Blackthorn, the whole town nearly dropped its collective teeth."

"She and Marcus seem made for each other."

"I couldn't agree more. I was sorry to hear that her mother died. That was a blow to Aurelia, especially with the trial and then finding the treasure. I think they said they were going to Spain on their honeymoon?"

"Spain," Rebecca agreed. "They're traveling without an itinerary. They said they'd check in, but that I was to handle whatever came up."

"May I make another trained observer comment?" Dru asked.

"Sure." Her face showed slight concern.

"You look up to the task."

She laughed again. "A comedian and a flatterer. I like them both."

"Well enough to have dinner with me tonight?" Dru was shocked at the words. Since he'd broken up with his girlfriend of five years, he hadn't even thought of dating. He knew too well the toll his job took on personal relationships, and he never wanted to go through the hardship of such a breakup again. Celeste was a great person. The fault had been in him and his total dedication to the law.

He could see that Rebecca was taken aback by his offer, and he wished he'd kept his mouth shut. Her blue eyes held his.

"Dinner would be nice," she said. "I guess I just assumed you were involved with someone."

"Is that a compliment?"

She laughed. "Perhaps. I'm not as free with them as you are."

"A challenge. I like that." He was feeling better about his offer now. Rebecca Barrett was quick-witted and beautiful. It was an evening he was looking forward to.

"Let me show you Joey's apartment."

She took him through the barn, her slim form preceding his as they examined the stalls and climbed to the loft. Still chatting easily, they walked back to Blackthorn and to the site where the framework of the new house stood in stark relief against the sky.

Dru looked to the west where he could see the broad band of the Mississippi River sweeping by. Just slightly south, downriver, was the town of Natchez. He loved this land, this area.

"You look like you've just found home," Rebecca said.

"Home in the sense of this whole county," Dru said, sweeping his hand to include the entire vista. "I've never aspired to owning Blackthorn, but I'm glad to be friends with the owners. I hope to be invited to dinner often."

Rebecca showed him the house plans. He spoke of the verandas and the plants, enthusiastic about the landscaping of the yard.

"You sound like you'd make a fair landscape architect if you ever decided to give up the law," Rebecca said.

"I was trained in that field. That was my career ambition, but my dad was sheriff, and when his health failed, I sort of inherited the office. Then I got elected," he said, shrugging, feeling the heat creep into his cheeks.

"And they just keep electing you," Rebecca said, grinning with a bit of an imp in her eyes.

"Something like that."

"You must do a good job."

"Now that's a matter of opinion, but I do love my work. Most of the time. There are always those hard cases when you have to prosecute someone you know and like. Thank goodness those don't happen often."

There was the sound of footsteps crunching on the gravel behind them and Marcus turned to see a man with angry gray eyes headed for them.

"I told you to keep that simpleton away from me. He's spilled a wheelbarrow of manure right in the middle of an excavation that took me three days."

Rebecca lifted an eyebrow. "Brett Gibson, this is Sheriff Dru Colson. Sheriff, Brett is working on the excavation of the Indian mound with some help from John Ittawasa."

Dru felt an instant dislike for Brett. Part of it was the man's arrogant demeanor, but the other part was the tiniest edge of contempt he leveled at Rebecca.

"Mr. Ittawasa isn't helping me," Brett snapped. "He's here to make sure no one steals any of the artifacts. Including me and my team."

"John is a good man," Dru said carefully. "He loves the history of his people far more than anyone else. I'm sure he's very excited to see what you find."

"Right," Brett said. "So what are you going to do about that—"

"Stop it, Brett. Don't say that word!"

Dru felt Rebecca tense beside him, and he was aware of her hands clenching. She wanted to slug the arrogant fool, and Dru thought he might help her.

"I've told you not to refer to Joey in those terms," she said evenly. "If he's made a mistake, I'll correct it."

"You'd better put a leash on that boy and keep him out of my way."

"Or what?" Dru asked conversationally, but with enough ice that it stopped Brett in his tracks. Dru saw his true colors. He'd rage and try to intimidate Rebecca, but he wouldn't stand up to Dru or what stood behind him—the law.

"Or nothing. I'll quit," Brett said.

"None of my business, but I have to point out that might not be such a bad idea," Dru said. Suddenly, he'd developed a case of loose tongue. Twice in the past half hour he'd said exactly what he was thinking.

Brett glared at the sheriff and walked away.

Rebecca turned to Dru with a rueful grin on her face. "He's good at his job, just a little prickly."

"Yes, something like that. He needs a few Southern manners."

"He's got a good crew, let me introduce you."

Dru followed Rebecca to the mound where three men were gently brushing dirt away from what looked like a series of clay vessels.

"Tony Wells, Rich Tanner, and Carlos Liotta," Rebecca said, introducing Dru. A woman carrying bottled water came trudging up the slope. "And this is—"

"Regina Batson," Dru said, smiling. "I saw your dad last week and he told me how proud he is that you're working with him. He said you were taking a break from school for a while but that you should have your degree soon."

"I helped with the design of the estate," Regina said, "and then I became interested in the dig. You know, everyone's heard about Blackthorn. Brett and Rebecca said I could help out with the excavation. Who knows, we might find more treasure." Her eyes crinkled with laughter.

"Yeah, we heard about that treasure. And we heard about the trouble out here before we came," Rich said, standing up. He was tall, lanky, and the sweat had soaked his hair so that it stuck to his face. "Do you suppose there's more treasure?"

Dru laughed. "Sorry boys, you're about three months too late."

Rich nodded. "Story of my life. Day late and a dollar short." He glanced around. "Still, no harm in looking, I suppose."

"Unfortunately, that's not true," Rebecca said instantly. "Brett is excavating the burial mound and that small area at the base of it. Digging elsewhere is prohibited."

Rich glanced at his two friends. "Whatever you say, boss lady." He grinned, and there was no malice in his tone.

"Thanks," Rebecca said. "I'm only following the directives given to me by the owners."

Dru took his farewells of the men and headed back to his patrol car. He'd been eager to get out of the sheriff's office when he'd taken the call to Blackthorn. It had been his best decision in weeks.

"Regina Batson is certainly an interesting addition to the team," Rebecca said lightly. "When she's around, Brett makes an effort not to be a total bear."

"Thank goodness someone has a positive effect on him." Dru shrugged one shoulder. "May I pick you up at seven?" he asked.

"Perfect. Casual?"

There was such hope in her voice that he laughed. "Casual it is. Seafood."

She smiled. "I'll be ready."

# CHAPTER TWO

REBECCA WAS GLAD she'd chosen the yellow sundress. Sitting on the dock of the restaurant with a gentle breeze from the Mississippi, she felt sexy and feminine. It was impossible not to, the way Dru Colson was looking at her.

"Why aren't you married?" Dru asked.

Rebecca laughingly held out her wrists. "Are you going to arrest me before you interrogate me?"

Dru laughed too, but a little self-consciously. "Sorry. I guess that did come out a little on the gruff side."

"Not gruff, just direct," Rebecca said. She bit her lip as she decided how much to tell him. "I was engaged. Last year. The wedding was planned, everything." She hesitated, but she could see in his eyes that he would ask. He wasn't a man who held back on the questions. "I cancelled the wedding, but Mike didn't object too strenuously. I think we'd both begun to see that we weren't meant for each other. We just wanted different things."

"Like children?" Dru asked.

"Yes."

"I know exactly how that goes," he said ruefully.

"Celeste, the woman I was involved with for five years, finally gave me the ultimatum—marriage and kids or she was leaving."

She could see that he still struggled with the loss. "Mike was the same way. He just couldn't believe that I didn't want to settle down and start a family."

Dru's eyebrows lifted. "*You* didn't want the children?"

"Yes, that's right." She couldn't help a wry grin as she realized how shocked he was. It was true. Most women wanted to start families when they were in their late twenties and early thirties. "It isn't that I don't like children, it's just that…" She broke it off. It was impossible to explain. Mike's mother had said she was unnatural. Mrs. Cuevas had been very angry with Rebecca, and she'd let everyone know it.

"Hey," Dru said, putting a hand on her shoulder. "You don't owe me an explanation. I understand. I love my nieces and nephews, but I'm just not ready to take on that responsibility. I don't know that I'll ever be, and I won't be railroaded into something that important to please someone else."

"Exactly!" Rebecca said, and she felt as if Dru did understand. She'd been the eldest of seven children, and all of her life had been spent taking care of others. Once she got out of college, she'd vowed to live her own life for at least fifteen years before she began living for someone else.

"Another drink?"

She looked at the empty Long Island iced tea glass.

The drinks were delicious, but potent. She'd never been one to deliberately set herself up for a headache. "Better not."

"Coffee?"

"That would be great." She found she wanted to linger on the restaurant's dock with Dru. They'd spent the entire evening talking about Natchez and Blackthorn and the mound-building Indians who were now the focus of Brett Gibson's research in Natchez.

As the waitress placed the coffee on the wrought-iron table, Rebecca refastened the elastic band around her honey-colored hair. She'd begun the evening with it down on her shoulders, but the wind whipping off the water had sent it flying. The only solution was scissors or restraint.

"This has been the most relaxing evening I've had in months," Dru said.

"Me, too. Thanks for asking me. Maybe Joey will let me borrow his newfangled kitchen to cook a meal for all of us."

"I'd like that," Dru said.

They sipped their coffee and let the warm night sounds drift around them. It was unusual to spend only one evening with a man and feel comfortable enough not to force the conversation. But Dru was different from most men she'd known. He had a quiet confidence that allowed her to relax—to drop the role of hostess and caretaker that had been hers since she was a child.

"Why don't we leave here and go under the hill?" Dru asked with a grin.

"Under the hill?" Rebecca wasn't certain what he was talking about. "A cave?"

"It's a part of town that used to be wide open. Sort of the French Quarter of Natchez," he said, "like the older part of New Orleans. Back in the days when Natchez was a booming river town, all of the best bars and gambling dens were located 'under the hill' or down on the water. It was a rowdy place known for its lawlessness and danger."

"Until you were elected sheriff?" she asked innocently.

"I'm not quite that old," he said, pretending to be wounded. "But if I can use my cane, I think I can dance a few numbers with you."

"I haven't danced in…a long time," Rebecca admitted. How long had it been? College? Surely not, but she couldn't recall another time.

"You don't forget," he said. "I have a dirty little secret to tell you if you agree to go."

"My, my, a lawman who bribes," she said. "Okay, let's go. You've got my curiosity working overtime." It was true. Just the hint of a secret was enough to whet her appetite. Dru was only jesting, but it was very effective.

They drove down a street that seemed to drop almost to the water's edge. As Dru parked the car, Rebecca could already hear the music and laughter coming from several restaurants and bars.

"Sounds young," she said, a little nervously. She wasn't thirty, yet she often felt much older.

"Not where we're going. That's my dirty secret. When

I broke up with Celeste, I was so depressed the deputies got together and paid for some ballroom dancing lessons. I discovered that I liked it."

"No!" Rebecca was shocked. Dru, in his cowboy boots and jeans didn't look a whit like someone who would tango or rumba. But then, what, exactly, would someone who could do those things look like? "I don't know how to do those dances," she said.

"Don't worry," he whispered. "I learned that the man's job is to make the woman look good."

They entered a restaurant and Dru led her down a flight of steps to a small bar where a woman in a sequined gown sang as a half dozen couples danced.

Before she could muster a protest, he pulled her into his arms and began waltzing her around the floor. "Relax," he said. "Just relax, feel the music and let me lead."

"Easier said than done," she said, trying so hard to relax that she made herself stiff all over again. But in a few moments, she picked up the rhythm. When she did so, Dru began to move more freely around the dance floor with her. After one or two faltering steps, she adapted to his lead. In only a few moments, they were dancing like old partners.

"See, I told you it's easy," he said, putting her into a turn and bringing her back into his arms.

"Only because you make it easy," she said, grinning widely. "This is great."

Dru ordered drinks, and they sipped them in between dancing each number. Rebecca was shocked when she looked down at her watch and saw that it was after two in the morning. "I should go home," she said a little breathlessly.

"Me, too," Dru said reluctantly. "The night just got away from us."

He was paying the tab when his cell phone rang. Frowning, he answered it, waving to Rebecca that he was going outside to talk. She should collect his change.

The expression on his face had her worried as she accepted the bills from the cashier and hurried up the steps and into the warm night.

"Ms. Barrett is with me," Dru was saying. "I'll escort her home and check it out. No, don't worry about it. You did the right thing by calling."

He put the phone away and turned to face her. "There's been some trouble at Blackthorn," he said. "I'll take you there right away."

DRU SAW the flashing lights of the ambulance and pulled up behind it. Beside him, Rebecca looked alabaster she was so pale. She didn't even wait for the car to stop. She got out and ran to the back of the ambulance where two attendants were loading Joey Reynolds.

"Joey," Rebecca said, grasping his hand. The young man was unconscious. "Joey!"

Dru put his hands on Rebecca's shoulders and gently moved her out of the way of the paramedics as they prepared Joey for transport to the hospital.

"What happened?" Rebecca asked two officers who were standing nearby.

They looked at Dru, and he nodded.

"We got a call that Mr. Reynolds had fallen from the loft of the barn. It seems he may have been haying the horses when he tripped. I can't guarantee it, ma'am, but he was breathing good and all. Once he regains consciousness, he's probably going to be okay."

Dru wanted to thank the man for his kindness. No one could guarantee Joey's condition, but the deputy had seen enough accidents to be able to deduce a little something to set Rebecca's mind at ease.

"Who called the ambulance?" she asked.

"I did." Brett stepped into the circle of light thrown by the patrol car headlights.

"Thanks, Brett," Rebecca said.

"Now maybe you'll listen to me and get that…Joey off the property. He's not responsible. He never should be allowed around those horses. Up in that barn fiddling around, nearly killing himself."

"Mr. Gibson," Dru stepped in. Now wasn't the time to rant and rave about what should have been done. "How do you know Joey tripped and fell?"

"I don't know for certain. Maybe Joey was trying to fly," he said sarcastically. "Either he tripped or he jumped, officer. I was giving him the benefit of the doubt."

"I should go to the hospital," Rebecca said. "When he wakes up, I want him to see someone familiar."

"I'll drive you," Dru offered.

"No, stay here and do what you can to find out what happened. I'll take my own car."

Dru didn't like her pale complexion, but he knew it was pointless to argue with her. He'd known enough women in his day to realize that trying to stop one on a chosen path was about as effective as stepping in front of a train. "I'll check with you as soon as I'm finished here," he promised and watched her hurry off into the night.

With his two deputies, Dru began to look around the barn area. He found where Joey had fallen, and when he looked, it did appear as if perhaps Joey had stumbled and fallen from the loft into the center aisle of the barn. That raised several questions, one of which he asked Brett.

"What was Joey doing in the hayloft at two in the morning?" Dru didn't mention that he'd known Joey all of his life. Joey was honest, hardworking and he slept the sleep of the innocent. He went to bed at ten and got up at dawn. He wasn't inclined to wandering around in the dark.

"I don't have a clue," Brett said in a snappy tone.

The anthropologist had a sharp tongue and an acid disposition. If he'd ever been taught any manners at all, he'd forgotten them.

"What were *you* doing wandering the premises at two in the morning?" Dru asked easily.

There was a pause as Brett considered the subtle implication that his early-morning wanderings might have some impact on Joey's. "I heard something," he said.

"I was asleep in my tent and I heard someone rustling around in the bushes. I got up to see who it was. Then I heard this moaning sound and I went to investigate. Instead of questioning me, you should be thanking me. If I hadn't stumbled on Joey, he'd have lain out there all night."

Dru didn't point out that it wasn't his job to thank someone for acting like a civilized human. "Do you think maybe Joey heard something, too?"

Brett rolled his eyes. "Joey's only interested in those damn horses and his plants. If the horses or plants were talking, he was probably out in the barn listening."

"Thank you," Dru said. He was tired and he had had just about as much of Brett Gibson as he could take. He spoke with the two deputies, and they began marking off the area. It looked like a simple accident, but where Blackthorn was concerned, Dru knew he couldn't be too careful.

Rebecca had seen someone in the woods that very morning. It was possible someone was on the property with the intention of making trouble.

WHEN JOEY OPENED his eyes, he blinked and focused on Rebecca. "I knew you'd help me," he said. "My head hurts."

"I know," Rebecca answered, sitting on the edge of the bed and taking his hand. No matter that the doctors had assured her he was fine. Now, with his gentle blue eyes focused on her, she could believe it. "You scared me half to death, Joey. You've been asleep for nearly twelve hours."

"Twelve hours?" he said, his forehead furrowing. "I'm sorry. I was scared."

"What happened?" Rebecca eased back, giving him some space.

"I was in my apartment," he said, "looking at some seed catalogues. I think snapdragons by the foundation of the house, don't you?"

"Perfect. What happened?"

"I heard someone in the barn."

The words chilled Rebecca so effectively that she had to remember to draw in a breath. "Who? Did you see anyone?"

Joey shook his head. "I slipped out of the apartment, hurried down the stairs, and then I thought I heard someone in the loft. So I went to the feed room and climbed the ladder there. I was afraid they'd try to hurt one of the horses, so I was really careful."

There was only one ladder into the loft. If someone was up there and Joey went looking, he'd essentially trapped that person.

"Did you see anyone?" Rebecca asked again.

"No. Someone hit me on the head with something. I lost my balance and fell."

Rebecca forced herself to take a deep breath. The worst thing she could do would be to frighten Joey with her own panic. "Are you sure someone hit you?" she asked gently.

Joey nodded. "Feel." He reached for her hand and put it on a big knot on the side of his head. "There."

"Joey, do you know who did this?"

He shook his head. "I didn't see who it was."

"Did you notice anything else?"

"There was a red can in the loft. It looked like the can that goes with the tractor."

"Diesel?" Rebecca couldn't hide her fear any longer. Was it possible someone intended to set the barn on fire and that by some fluke Joey had prevented it?

"Yeah, the diesel for the tractor. It looked like that can, but it shouldn't have been in the barn. It belongs in the equipment shed."

"That's right," Rebecca said, eager to get to the court-house and check with Dru to see what he'd found.

"Did I do the right thing?" Joey asked, a frown on his face. "I don't want to disappoint Aurelia and Marcus. They said I should watch out for the horses and all the animals at Blackthorn."

"You did exactly right," Rebecca reassured him, squeezing his hand. "You did perfect, Joey. Now I'm going in to talk with the sheriff. Will you be okay?"

He nodded. "Can I go home soon?"

"As soon as they release you," Rebecca said. "I'll be back for you."

Before she was at the door he had closed his eyes and had drifted into sleep. She watched from the doorway for a moment, wondering just how lucky he'd been to escape with his life.

WHEN SHE ARRIVED at the courthouse, she wasn't surprised to see that Dru was in his office. It wasn't quite noon yet, but the courthouse was emptying out. She walked into the sheriff's office and saw Drew, backlit by a large window in his private office.

"How's Joey?" he asked, his gaze lingering on her.

"He's going to be okay. He said someone hit him."

Dru stood up and walked around, assisting Rebecca into a chair. "I wish I had better news. We found a piece of lumber with blood and hair on it that I'm positive will be Joey's. Someone struck him with that lumber."

"And deliberately knocked him out of the loft? They could easily have killed him."

"I can't speak to their intention, but they surely meant to knock him out."

"Joey said there was a can of diesel in the loft."

Dru's eyebrows shot up. "We searched the loft but we didn't find any diesel fuel."

"Maybe Joey frightened them away."

"If he did, he's a very lucky man to be alive. And so are those horses."

"What's going on, Dru?" Rebecca asked, trying hard not to let her voice tremble.

"I don't know, but we're going to find out."

## CHAPTER THREE

BRETT AND THE rest of the crew were drinking the last of the iced tea from their lunch break when Rebecca got back to Blackthorn.

"How is Joey?" Brett asked, and there was an odd tone in his voice.

Rebecca felt a sudden chill. Brett hated Joey, but surely not enough to try and injure him.

"He's going to be okay. He's very lucky. The fall from the barn could have killed him."

"I know you think I'm a hard man," Brett said, "but Joey shouldn't be out here. This is a dangerous place and he's going to get hurt."

Rebecca locked her gaze with Brett's and spoke softly. "Joey didn't trip and fall. Someone hit him with a board and tried to kill him."

Brett's face drew into a frown. "That's nuts. Who would want to hurt the simpleton?"

"That's a good question," Rebecca said. "And I'm sure Sheriff Colson will find the answer to it."

"Who would want to hurt Joey?" Brett repeated almost as if he were talking to himself.

"Don't repeat that information to the rest of the crew," Rebecca cautioned him.

"Because you're afraid they'll quit?"

"Because one of them may have done it," Rebecca said, once again watching Brett for any sign of guilt.

"I've worked with these men on two other digs." Brett was having no difficulty working himself into indignation. "They have no reason to injure Joey."

It was interesting that Brett defended his men. Rebecca took it as a good sign. "Nonetheless, it's best if they don't know that Joey was attacked. The construction workers are also going to be questioned. If someone on the estate is guilty, it'll be easier to find out who it is if they don't think we're suspicious."

"Except it puts my workers in some jeopardy," Brett pointed out. "They have a right to know that someone is on the loose at Blackthorn, whacking people in the head."

Rebecca felt her throat close. She hadn't said that Joey was hit in the head. "Brett, don't argue with me. Just do what I tell you. In the end, I'm the one responsible, not you." She walked away, hoping that her little act of bravado had covered her intense concern about Brett and his involvement with what had happened to Joey. As soon as she got a chance to talk to Dru, she'd repeat the entire conversation.

Although she was tired, she knew she wouldn't be able to rest. She went up to the shell of the house. Progress was being made, but it seemed slow to her.

The contractor had built a makeshift staircase to the

upper floor, and though she'd given strict orders to all but the carpenters not to venture to the upper levels, she climbed up herself.

The vista was incredible. The house Aurelia and Marcus were building wasn't huge—at least not like the former plantation that had stood on Blackthorn. But it was an imposing structure that seemed to rise from the high bluff overlooking the river. The exterior walls would be made of cement blocks poured in specially designed molds to give the appearance of limestone. Once finished, the house would be indestructible. Those inside the walls of Blackthorn House would have the most spectacular view of the Mississippi in the whole area.

Leaning against a four-by-four support, Rebecca gazed down at the early sunlight on the "father of waters," as the Indians had called the Mississippi.

Movement at the base of the cliff caught her eye. Probably a deer. She leaned out, trying to get a good look. She caught only a glimpse, but something about what she saw troubled her. There was too much white for a deer. The animal she saw moved in a jerky fashion, not with the smooth, bounding grace of a whitetail.

The man burst out of a clump of shrubs and darted into another. He was almost at the river, and when he got there, he looked in both directions before dragging a small boat out of the bush and jumping into it. In a matter of moments, he was swirling away in the current.

"Damn!" Rebecca watched as he disappeared in the

tree-covered lee of the river. She left the window and hurried back to the caretaker's cottage. It was too late to catch whoever was on Blackthorn property illegally, but maybe they'd left some clues behind.

DRU WAS pleasantly surprised when the telephone rang on his desk at three forty-five and he heard Rebecca's breathless voice. He'd just been thinking of her. But when she reported what she'd seen, he told her to hold on, he was on the way.

The two deputies who'd worked the assault on Joey were off duty, so Dru called two others to work the physical evidence at the riverbank, if there was any.

He didn't wait for them to get their gear. He got in his car and drove straight to Blackthorn. Rebecca looked both excited and tired, and he had to stop himself from the impulse to put his arms around her.

"It was directly below the house," she said, starting toward the river.

Dru didn't have to wait long for his men. They pulled up and began to ease down the steep bluff that over-looked the powerful river.

"Should we go with them?" Rebecca asked.

Dru shook his head. "The best thing we can do is stay out of their way. If they find something, they'll let me know."

"I can't help but wonder who's trespassing so freely on Blackthorn," Rebecca said. "I saw him. He's slender with sandy-brown hair. And he seems to know his way around here fairly well."

"I talked to Joey," Dru said. "He just didn't see anyone. He's eager to come home, though."

Rebecca rubbed her right eyebrow with her finger. "Brett says it isn't safe for Joey here. He says Joey's going to get hurt." She met Dru's gaze. "And that it would be my fault if I allowed him to stay in a dangerous place."

Dru shook his head lightly. "Joey's a grown man, Rebecca. He's a little slow, but he knows Blackthorn better than anyone else. He's as safe here as anywhere else."

"What about last night?"

"The person who struck Joey wasn't lying in wait for him. Joey interrupted something. And in all likelihood saved the lives of those three horses."

Rebecca couldn't deny that. "I just don't want him hurt. He's such a kind man…."

"And one who knows how to keep his eyes open now that he's aware of danger."

Rebecca's smile was like the sun slipping out from behind a cloud. "You make me feel better, you know."

"You don't deserve to feel bad," he said simply.

"I wonder what's going on here?" Rebecca said. "The treasure has been found. There's no reason for anyone else to be slipping through the woods, causing trouble."

"But someone is—or at least someone is slipping through the woods," Dru pointed out, wondering himself if there were two separate incidents—the attack on Joey and some kids trespassing on Blackthorn for a thrill. He wasn't so certain the "trespasser" was harmless.

The two deputies came up from the bluff. "We got a cast of a footprint," one said, "but that's about it. A male. About a size 11, worn running shoes. It's distinctive if we can find the shoe. There's a small place on the bank where someone's been tying up a boat. It's been used more than once."

Dru nodded. "Good work."

"Can you recommend a good security agency?" Rebecca asked. "I'll hire a watchman to guard that landing."

One thing Dru liked about Rebecca was her ability to land on her feet. When something happened, she figured out a way to fix it. But he wasn't ready yet to post a guard.

"If we're lucky, the intruder isn't aware that he's been seen. He didn't see you in the scaffolding, did he?"

Rebecca shook her head, her expression showing curiosity about where he was going.

"Then he may believe he hasn't been discovered at the landing. If that's true, he'll come back."

"Which is exactly why I want someone down there to stop him."

"But it may be our best opportunity to catch him," Dru said with a grin. "If we're waiting for him up here."

He saw the two deputies look at each other. The glance was covert, and in an instant they were impassive again. Rebecca obviously saw it too.

"I doubt the Adams County Sheriff's Department will stake out my property to prevent a trespasser," she said.

"I couldn't assign one of my men," Dru agreed. "But I could stay myself. I think a night watch will be sufficient."

He saw the unexpected rush of gratitude on Rebecca's face and realized she would never have asked for special favors. That was another thing he liked about her. She didn't assume anything.

"I'd rather catch him than scare him off," Rebecca admitted. "I'm afraid if he gets scared off the river, he'll just come in from the road."

"I suspect you're right about that," Dru agreed, meeting his deputies' amused glances.

"I'll volunteer to help, too," one of the deputies said with a wicked grin at Dru. "Me, too," the other chimed in.

"All I can say is that the Adams County law enforcement is the most accommodating I've ever heard about," Rebecca said. "Perhaps I could offer you gentlemen some coffee and breakfast?"

"If you're sure it's no bother," Dru said, shaking his head in amusement at his two officers.

As he and Rebecca led the way to the cottage, he glanced back toward the river. Who was on Blackthorn property and what were they doing there? With the recovery of the treasure and Marcus's confession that he'd been playing the role of Andre Agee, the mysterious horseman, to thwart development of the property,

Dru had hoped that all of the rumors and odd events at Blackthorn would stop. Now it looked as if he'd been more than a tiny bit optimistic.

REBECCA SLIPPED into her riding breeches with a sigh of guilty anticipation. She'd brought Joey home from the hospital with a knot the size of a goose egg on his head, but the doctor had assured her he was perfectly fine. She'd left him sitting in the shade of a big pecan, watching over his garden.

She'd talked to the contractor, Eugene Batson, about the wiring, repeating all of the things Marcus had written on a list for her. One thing she'd learned from this experience was that she never wanted to build a house. The details were endless, and there were times she simply had to guess what Marcus and Aurelia would want. Perhaps the experience would be more enjoyable if she weren't serving as absentee owner. Then again, how many people got to participate in the construction of what was going to be one of the most architecturally innovative houses ever built. She grinned as she laced her paddock boots.

For the time being, though, she could simply put all of that aside for an hour and enjoy a ride on Cogar.

Joey was drawing another diagram of a garden in the dirt, but he promised her he wouldn't get hot working. She winked at him as she went on to the barn and saddled the big gray. Cogar was so tall, she almost needed a mounting block to get on. Almost.

When she was in the saddle, he moved out willingly,

as eager for the ride as she was. As soon as she was in the woods, she let her troubles slip away. They walked until he was warm, moved into a trot, then eased into a ground-covering gallop. Her mind slipped to fantasy.

As a young girl, she'd often fantasized about Robin Hood and Sherwood Forest. That's what the woods around Blackthorn reminded her of. At any moment the band of merry robbers could step out of the woods.

She smiled at a childhood memory: she'd been torn between wanting to be Robin—or Maid Marian. Robin seemed to have the most fun, but Marian was certainly beautiful. Those thoughts led her to Dru. He was a handsome man with a casual grace and easy confidence that she found delightful. Since he was so secure in who he was, she didn't feel any pressure from him to change who she was. Of course, they were just getting to know each other. In the beginning, Mike had been easygoing, too. It was only toward the end that he began to act as though her hopes and dreams didn't matter. What he wanted was the only important thing.

As if her thoughts precipitated it, a dark cloud covered the sun, casting the woods in shadow. Cogar had slowed to a walk, and Rebecca felt a little foolish as chill bumps danced over her arms.

Cogar's head lifted, his ears pricked forward. Then she heard it. The sound of a baby crying. It was the eeriest thing she'd ever heard, rising and falling in desperate bursts from somewhere in the woods. Everything that Aurelia had told her came back to her.

Yvonne Harris and Randall Levert had been playing

tape recordings of a crying baby in the woods of Blackthorn in an attempt to frighten Aurelia off the estate. And then Yvonne had taken it several steps further. She'd murdered Randall's mother, Lottie, and tried to pin the murder on Aurelia by planting evidence. She'd also betrayed her co-conspirator by planting evidence against him, too. She'd intended to get both Aurelia and Randall out of the way.

Fortunately, Yvonne's plans had been foiled. Aurelia, though charged, had been found innocent of Lottie Levert's murder. Yvonne had been found guilty of Lottie's death and was in the state penitentiary.

Randall, shocked that his partner in crime had murdered his own mother in an attempt to frame him, had turned state's evidence against Yvonne. He, too, was serving time.

So why was a baby crying in the woods at Blackthorn, in some eerie repetition of past events?

Cogar stepped forward, as if he wanted to go into the woods. Rebecca reined him in. She sat and listened, the sound of the baby almost breaking her heart. But she wasn't going into the woods. There were trespassers on Blackthorn and she was smart enough not to walk into a trap. If someone was playing tricks on her, she wouldn't fall for them. Instead, she'd go straight back to the cottage and call Dru.

She had no belief that the baby crying in the woods was real. Therefore she didn't feel it necessary to try and find it. Nudging Cogar into a trot, she headed back to the cottage and a telephone.

DRU FROWNED as he hung up the receiver. It wasn't what he called justice, but then, he'd learned that when a witness cut a deal, lots of things were possible. He stared at the notes he'd made on a pad.

Randall Levert had been released from prison two days before based on the deal he'd cut with the prosecutor in testifying against Yvonne.

Dru wasn't happy with that information, but he knew that Randall hadn't been involved in his mother's murder. What he'd done was attempt to frighten Aurelia into selling Blackthorn. And he'd used poor judgment in teaming up with Yvonne Harris.

And it would seem that he was using poor judgment once again. Dru stood up. He had no doubt that the sudden "intruder" at Blackthorn was none other than Randall Levert. But why Randall would risk losing his probation was what troubled Dru. He was either stupid or crazy, and both of those mindsets could be very dangerous under the right circumstances.

Dru drove out to Blackthorn and caught sight of Rebecca trotting out of the woods on a huge gray horse. The sight was breathtaking. He'd never been overly interested in horses, but the sight of Rebecca astride the gray made the sport seem infinitely more fascinating.

The expression on her face, though, told another story. He was out of the patrol car and at her side in a flash.

"What's wrong?"

"There's a baby crying in the woods," she said, her voice trembling.

Dru realized she was more unnerved than she wanted him to know. His hand went to her knee in a gesture of comfort. "That stands to reason. They released Randall Levert on probation two days ago," he said, "just about the time someone started trespassing on Blackthorn property. What surprises me is that he's stupid enough to try the same stunt twice in a row."

"Why is he doing this?" Rebecca asked, and Dru was relieved to hear anxiety beginning to turn to anger.

"That's a good question. He's risking real jail time for this stunt."

"You're positive the person doing this is Randall Levert?"

Dru considered the question. His gut told him it was Randall, but there wasn't any evidence. "Fairly certain, but that doesn't mean I'll rule out other possibilities. What I am going to do is pick Randall up for questioning. If this is his idea of revenge, I'll make him understand he's playing a foolish game with severe consequences."

"I'm sorry this thing has just…exploded," Rebecca said. "First the man in the woods, then Joey, then the boat thing, and now the baby is back. I feel responsible for this in some way." She started to swing from the saddle.

Dru found his hands around her waist steadying her as she dropped to the ground. He half expected her to step away from him. Instead, she turned so that she was in the circle of his arms. Her blue eyes held his, and he let his hands remain on her waist.

"You have nothing to do with Randall and whatever sick plan he's hatched," Dru said, his gaze slipping to her mouth. It was full and looked soft. He imagined what it would feel like to kiss her. He wanted to. He watched her swallow and realized that she, too, was thinking of a kiss.

"Will you really come by tonight?" she asked.

"Yes," he said. "I'd feel better if I kept an eye on things."

"I'll make dinner for you," she said. "I'm a pretty good cook."

"A woman with endless talents," he said, knowing that the moment for the kiss had passed. But there would be other opportunities in the coming night, when he wasn't on duty and when Brett Gibson and the Batson girl weren't standing at the edge of the clearing watching them.

# CHAPTER FOUR

REBECCA BASTED the turkey breast for the last time and turned the oven off. She'd made a light salad and bought some fresh pears and blueberries. It was only May, but it was summertime in Natchez, far too hot for a heavy meal.

She checked her reflection in the bathroom mirror one more time, a little amused at herself for the mascara and lipstick she'd applied. Working out-of-doors, she normally didn't wear makeup. But there was something about Dru Colson that reminded her all too much of her femininity. Rebecca had tried on several outfits before she settled on one—atypical behavior yet again. She was getting into her "courting finery," as her Aunt Mildred would have said.

That, in and of itself, was a minor miracle. After her breakup with Mike, she'd never expected to find herself in a position of *wanting* to attract a man. She didn't dress to repel men, she just didn't think about it. But Dru Colson was different. He made her think about her appearance and his reaction to her. Surprisingly, it was nice to wonder what effect a sleeveless, sexy blouse would have on a man. Somehow, Dru made it seem so natural.

He was different from other men she'd known. Or so he seemed, she reminded herself. She hardly knew him. She didn't want to find herself out of the frying pan and into the fire. She was going to take things slowly.

She heard the sound of his car and felt her heart stutter. She ordered herself to take deep breaths, to go slow. Her heartbeat was accelerating and she could feel anticipation in every inch of her body. So much for speed limits. But when she opened the door of Joey's apartment to his knock, she was in perfect control.

"I drove around the perimeter of the property and everything seemed okay." His eyes crinkled into a smile as his gaze swept down her body, leaving a burning tingle behind. "You look lovely. And something smells wonderful."

"Thanks." Desire swept through her. "You look very handsome yourself." And he did, with his dark hair combed back and his clean-shaven, chiseled jaw so lean and tanned. There was no denying it. Dru was a well-built man. What her Aunt Mildred would call a Tilt-a-Whirl, so named after the dizzying amusement park ride.

"Joey should be here soon," Rebecca said. "He was delighted to let me use the new oven. I think even Joey gets tired of peanut butter and jelly sandwiches."

"I do," Joey said, coming in the door with a grin. His head was still bandaged, but he had a great appetite and said he felt fine.

"I checked the horses," he said, his mouth turning down at the corners. "I think we should let them out in the pasture and not keep them in the barn tonight."

Rebecca knew Joey was afraid someone would try to burn the barn again. "I think that's a good idea," she said. "We'll turn Cogar and Mariah out in the pasture right beside the barn and Diable in his paddock. You can hear them all night long."

"That does sound like a good plan," Dru agreed. "Joey, have you thought any more about who hit you?"

He nodded. "But I didn't see him. I've tried and tried to remember, but he was hiding and then he hit me and I fell."

"We'll figure it out," Dru reassured Joey as he glanced at Rebecca.

She nodded slightly. Both she and Dru had agreed that Joey needed to know that Randall Levert was out of jail on probation. She stood beside Joey's chair as Dru told him.

"He'll come back here," Joey said, and he turned to look up at Rebecca with worry in his eyes. "He's a mean man. Why did they let him out of jail? He wants to hurt me and he'll hurt you, too."

"Randall Levert won't be bothering anyone if he has a lick of sense. I'll have a talk with him tomorrow," Dru said. "I can't guarantee that he won't come here, but I can make him understand that he'll be in serious trouble if he does."

"He was so mad," Joey said, his voice tight with

worry. "He wanted everyone to think Aurelia had killed his mother. Then when it was Yvonne, he was even madder."

"I know," Rebecca said, putting a hand on Joey's shoulder. "But we're all here together. Remember, Brett and his crew are camping by the burial mound. I'm here and Dru is going to stay around. Randall won't come here. There are too many people on the property now."

"I hope not." Joey didn't sound reassured. "He's mean."

"Joey, I want you to keep your eyes and ears open," Dru said. "If you see anything funny, you call me, okay?"

"Aurelia and Marcus gave me a cell phone," he said, pulling it out of his pocket. "So I can call for help any time I need it."

Dru examined the phone that Joey held out to him. "That's a great idea. So you call if you see or hear anything, okay? You can help me protect Rebecca."

"And the horses," Joey said.

"And the horses," Rebecca agreed.

She put the food on the table and they ate, chatting about Joey's garden and how Brett and his crew had unearthed an intact vessel that contained what appeared to be even more valuable artifacts. The fact that the earthen vessel was still unbroken after so many years was a minor miracle in itself.

"John Ittawasa is coming tomorrow," Rebecca said. "I called him and reported the find, just as Aurelia

promised we would do. I'm afraid it's going to be another battle with Brett." She sighed. "John wants to take
the artifacts back to Philadelphia, Mississippi, and have
them documented at the Choctaw Indian Reservation.
Brett wants to keep them here so he can study them and
perhaps do an exhibit at a later date. I see both points
of view."

"If John documents them, perhaps he'll allow Brett
to use them later, when he has a more complete collec-
tion," Dru said.

"Oh, that voice of reason just isn't heard in the heat
of the argument. Believe me, I've tried to reason with
Brett. He's totally in a snit."

"Who has the final say?" Dru asked.

Rebecca looked into his eyes. "I do."

"What are you going to do?" Dru asked.

"I haven't made up my mind yet."

"May I offer some advice?" Dru asked.

"I'd love it, though I can't promise to take it." She
would be glad to hear advice from an unbiased party,
especially one as level-headed as Dru.

"I wouldn't keep the artifacts on Blackthorn property
no matter who ultimately has control of them. You've
been having trouble. It would be a crying shame if someone came in and destroyed these artifacts in some act
of vengeance or revenge."

Rebecca took a deep breath. "Thanks, Dru. That's the
best reasoning I've heard. You make perfect sense, and
I'll make sure the artifacts are put somewhere safe. Like
a bank vault or something, first thing in the morning."

"How valuable are these things?" Dru asked.

"Depends on who you ask. So little is known about the Mound Builders that this may be the definitive site. They lived along the Mississippi River, and there were more burial mounds until the river broke the levee in 1927 and flooded most of the delta. A lot of history, both Native American and early settler, was lost then. If this is the most preserved site, then the artifacts are quite valuable from a historical perspective."

"What about jewels and gold and things like that?"

"Not really a part of the Mound Builders' interest. The Aztecs and Toltecs in South America actually made gold jewelry and adorned themselves with silver and gold. Around here there weren't a lot of precious metals or jewels."

"So what's the monetary value of this site?"

"I'm not sure that's easy to explain. Most people think only of jewels and precious metals when it comes to tombs. The pyramids in Egypt were filled with material wealth. This site is different. Brett has schooled me well," she said, giving an apologetic grin. "This site is about information, history, preservation of a site sacred to Native American Indians. And," she got a teasing look in her eyes, "Brett says there's some indication that Ponce de Leon had begun to believe that the fountain of youth was somewhere along the great Mississippi River."

"Ah, the old fountain-of-youth lure."

"Now to find evidence of that would be valuable information. *Monetarily* valuable information."

"Even more valuable would be to find the fountain of youth," Dru teased. "Can you imagine? You could charge five dollars an ounce and become a gazillionaire overnight."

"Not me. Aurelia and Marcus," Rebecca reminded him. "I'm just the hired help and I'm the one who's going to have to deal with Brett about that artifact."

Joey touched Rebecca's arm. "Brett said it was wrong to give the old bowl to the Indian," Joey said. "He said he wasn't going to do it."

Rebecca felt a flush touch her cheeks. Brett talked big, but when it came time to yield up the artifacts, he would do so. He was a troublemaker, but he wasn't an idiot. Still, she didn't like the fact that he made her look foolish in front of people. He constantly challenged her authority and her decisions.

"I wouldn't put a lot of stock in what Brett says," Rebecca said easily. "All talk, no action."

She cleared the table and then served the orange sherbet she'd bought.

"Cool," Joey said, grinning. "Maybe I could grow some oranges."

"Maybe," she said because she didn't know if he could or not. The Natchez winters could get pretty cold.

"Strawberries might be better," Dru suggested.

"Yeah, strawberries." Joey stood up, his bowl empty. "I'm going to draw out some beds for strawberries. I know just where to put them."

He hurried out of the kitchen, leaving Dru and Rebecca alone. Together they cleaned up, working as a team as though they'd been doing it for years.

"Shall I walk you home?" Dru asked once they'd finished. His question sounded as if he was about fourteen years old.

"Only if you carry my books," Rebecca replied.

Chuckling softly, they left the apartment and started walking down the drive to the old caretaker's cottage. Rebecca was hyperaware of Dru. Though he didn't touch her, she felt electric.

The night was magnificent. Pale moonlight filtered through the old oaks draped with Spanish moss. There was a soft murmur, which Rebecca took to be the river. Around them the night had fallen silent, peaceful, serene.

They were almost at the caretaker's cottage, both still silent, when the sound of a crying baby seemed to come from nowhere—and everywhere.

"Go inside," Dru said softly, indicating the caretaker's cottage. "Lock the door, Rebecca."

"But—"

"No buts. Someone's out here."

"I'll come with you," she said, suddenly aware of the gun that had materialized in his hand.

"No, stay inside and lock the door. Don't come out."

He wasn't asking her, he was telling her. She slipped away from his side, over the porch and into the cottage. She knew enough not to flip on the light as she watched Dru disappear into the shadows of the trees, a shadow himself, but one moving fast and holding a deadly weapon.

MORE THAN DANGER, Dru felt total aggravation. He had no doubt that Randall Levert was behind all of this. Randall. A total idiot. The man had skated out of prison because of his willingness to rat out his partner. Now that he'd gained his freedom, he should be smart enough to stay away from Blackthorn and his foolish pranks.

Dru slipped into the woods. It was almost impossible to tell what direction the crying was coming from. Sound echoed and reverberated against the huge old trees. Pausing to listen, he thought he heard someone running fast through the underbrush.

He gave chase, ignoring the tiny limbs that whipped against his arms and face. He kept his attention focused solely on the sounds of the running person.

He thought he'd lost the runner, but then he heard a twig snap to his right. The intruder was much closer than Dru had thought. He bolted right just as someone ran out from beneath a huge wild magnolia. The bright moonlight came through a hole in the canopy of tree limbs, illuminating the runner's pale shirt.

"Police!" Dru called. "Halt! Police! Stop, or I'll shoot."

Damn! The guy took off sprinting again.

Dru turned on the speed, his own body skimming over the fallen limbs and trees and tangle of briars. He'd been a long-distance track runner in high school, and he'd kept up his running habits as part of his regimen. Although the woods were an aggravation, he could see that he was gaining on the man.

"Halt!" he called again. "I'm going to shoot."

When the man gave no indication of slacking his pace, Dru shot. There was an explosion of bark just above the runner's head and the man came to a screeching halt. By the time Dru got to him, he was standing with his hands over his head, his chest heaving.

The crying of the baby had ceased.

"You're under arrest for trespassing, among other things," Dru said as he walked up and patted the man down.

"I'm not trespassing," the man said. "Who the hell are you?"

"Sheriff Dru Colson, and you're under arrest. These woods are private property. They're also not the place for foolish practical jokes involving crying babies."

"I know, man, that nearly freaked me out. But I'm not trespassing. I work for Brett Gibson. I'm his dig coordinator."

Dru frowned and stepped back. "You're what?"

"The dig coordinator. At a dig, a lot of different sites get going sometimes. Someone has to coordinate all the levels, mark all the artifacts that are dug up and generally make sure the different strata of the dig are marked and examined. You know, it's happened before that someone planted valuable artifacts in a mound, hoping to claim some kind of government benefit. I'm here to make sure that doesn't happen."

Dru hesitated. The man sounded as if he knew what he was talking about. But it didn't make sense that he'd run. "Why did you run?"

"Man, I thought you were the dude who's been sneaking around. I was trying to get ahead so I could ambush you and tackle you, but you were too fast."

"What's your name?"

"Winston West. Folks call me Double-U. Uh, can I put my hands down now? I've got identification in my pocket."

"I can't see it here anyway," Dru said, motioning him to put his hands down. "We'll go back to camp and see if Brett will vouch for you."

"Good idea, man. I was afraid you were gonna plug me full of holes."

Dru cast a glance back through the woods. He'd caught the man he was chasing, but it didn't seem to be the right man. Dru had the distinct sense that someone was watching him. Watching and waiting for an opportunity to do something bad. Something that would certainly harm Rebecca.

"Did you see anyone else in the woods?" Dru asked.

"No. I just came over here to, you know, relieve myself. We'd been drinking a few beers. Anyway, I heard that baby. I almost jumped out of my pants. So I started running towards the sound, thinking it was a real baby. Then I got to thinking a real baby would be exhausted and stop crying, even for a few breaths. So then I decided to try to find whatever was playing the sound. That's when I heard you and I thought you might be the guy responsible. Like I said, I meant to run ahead of you and find a place to set up an ambush but you were too fast for me."

"This story had better check out," Dru warned him.

"Hey, man, I'm cool. Ask Brett."

Dru did just that, and Brett confirmed everything Winston West had said.

"There've been a series of accidents around Blackthorn," Dru said loudly enough for Brett and those of his assistants who were around to hear. "My suggestion to all of you is that once night falls, stay in the campsite. Stay where other members of your party can see you. If you need an alibi, then you'll have one."

"An alibi for what?" Brett asked. "What are you implying about me and my men?"

"Not a thing," Dru said softly. "I'm just giving you a tip, Gibson. Take it or leave it, I don't care."

"You should be chasing down whoever started that crying-baby noise," Brett said irritably. "Instead, you're courting Rebecca and harassing my workmen."

Dru didn't miss the fact that Brett, despite the way he spoke to Rebecca, seemed jealous of anyone else's attention to her. Well, stranger things had happened.

"Where is the artifact you dug up today?" Dru asked.

"Has she told *everyone?* Ms. Barrett would do well to learn to keep her mouth shut."

Dru felt a flash of anger. Brett was an egotist and an

ass. Dru took a deep breath and forced the anger out of his voice. "Where is the artifact?"

"In a very safe place," Brett said.

"Where?"

"In my tent," Brett said finally and with great reluctance. "No one goes in my tent."

"May I see it?" Dru asked, knowing that he'd get an argument. Brett was just that kind of man.

"You have no need to see it. It won't mean a thing to someone uneducated in—"

"Show it to me," Dru said levelly.

"If you insist!" Brett led the way to his tent. He went inside and in a moment, there was the sound of an exclamation. "No!" he cried, coming out of the tent in a rush. "It's gone."

"Gone?" Dru asked, his gaze narrowing on Brett's shocked expression. He didn't trust Brett as far as he could throw him. It occurred to him that the entire crying-baby thing could simply have been a diversion for Brett to steal the artifact so he didn't have to give it to John Ittawasa.

"It's gone!" Brett snapped. "Do something. You're the law around here. Do your job. Take some prints. Find out who stole that vessel."

"It's going to be a long night," Dru said, starting to walk away. "Don't go in that tent and don't let anyone else near it."

"What are you going to do? Where are you going?" Brett demanded.

"To call for backup and to check on Rebecca." He picked up his pace. He suddenly had a very bad feeling that he shouldn't have left her.

# CHAPTER FIVE

REBECCA LISTENED to the sound of the wailing baby and wanted to cover her ears. It was far worse in reality than it had been in her imagination when Aurelia had told her about it. Even though Rebecca knew it wasn't a real baby but some type of recording, it didn't stop the haunting sadness of the sound.

Why would Randall Levert be such an idiot that he would return to Blackthorn and try to play the crying-baby scam again? The obvious answer was that Randall had gone over the deep end. His mother had been murdered on Blackthorn property by his own partner, a Realtor named Yvonne Harris. Where Yvonne had been sentenced to prison for murder, Randall had turned state's evidence against her and had gotten himself a deal from the prosecutor. His involvement in the crime had been minimal—trying to frighten Aurelia away from Blackthorn. Randall was as much a victim of Yvonne as Aurelia had been. Maybe even more since he'd lost his mother to Yvonne's greed.

All of that said, it made Randall's determination to scuttle around Blackthorn even more creepy. He was unbalanced, and in a way that boded only ill for her and her project. But Dru would handle it. She thanked her lucky stars for the lawman, realizing that the baby's cries had ceased.

For a moment her thoughts slipped to Dru Colson. He was almost the antithesis of what she'd come to imagine a Mississippi sheriff might be. Of course, she did have an active imagination! But Dru was calm and deliberate. Handsome in a lean, athletic way. He was a man who'd taken up the badge not because he wanted the power but because he'd been asked. And asked again. He was young to bear the load of responsibility he shouldered, but he seemed born to it.

That was an interesting phrase. Born to it. Funny, but when she'd first met Aurelia Agee, she'd instantly known that Aurelia had been born to be heiress of Blackthorn. After five minutes of conversation with Aurelia and Marcus, Rebecca had been able to hook on to their vision and dream of what Blackthorn was in the past and what it could be in the future.

Aurelia had been able to convey that vision to Eugene Batson and his brother Roy, and together they'd come up with a house plan that was going to dazzle the architectural world. It was a heady time for Rebecca, spoiled only by some nutcase running through the woods with a taped recording of a crying baby. It would be funny if only someone hadn't attacked Joey and injured him. Concern for Joey made her start toward the door.

The tap on her door almost made her jump out of her skin. Caution made her stop before she removed the sliding chain lock.

"Rebecca? It's me, Regina."

Surprised, Rebecca opened the door to the young woman. A shaft of moonlight fell across the porch, illuminating Regina's pale blond hair.

"I came to get you," Regina said. "Brett is about to have a fit and the sheriff is calling for deputies."

"What happened?" Rebecca asked. Sudden concern made her legs seem a little heavy.

"I don't know for certain, but I think someone stole the artifact Brett found today."

"Damn!" Rebecca rarely resorted to profanity, but this was the worst thing that could happen on her watch. Aurelia had cautioned her about theft, and even Dru had had the foresight to see that artifacts from the burial mound might draw a thief's attention. She hadn't acted quickly enough to protect the valuable bowl.

She stepped onto the porch. "Let's go check it out."

"I didn't want to trouble you, but I thought you should know and no one else came to tell you."

Rebecca cast a look at Regina. Was she trying to tell Rebecca something or was she just nervous? She started to ask but stopped when she saw Dru jogging toward her.

"Are you okay?" he asked, putting his hands on her arms and moving them up and down as if to make certain with his touch.

"Fine. What happened?"

He told her about the theft, adding that he'd know more once the crime scene was fully examined. "I know you aren't going to like this, but I want everyone on the property rounded up and contained until I can go through their things and interview them."

"I don't like it, but I know it's necessary. We can all go back down to the cottage," Rebecca said. "I'll get Joey."

"I'm going with you," Regina said, obviously unwilling to be alone in the night with a burglar about.

By the time Rebecca roused Joey and made it back to the cottage with him and Regina, Brett and his crew were there and tension electrified the air.

"That cornpone sheriff has a lot of nerve herding us in here like a bunch of common thieves," Brett started as soon as Rebecca walked in the door.

"I'll make us some coffee," Rebecca offered, ignoring Brett's complaints. It was going to be a long night.

"Whoever stole that artifact is getting away while Deputy Dog is going through our personal stuff and wasting time."

Rebecca put on the kettle and got out some milk to make Joey a cup of cocoa. Her mind whirled with anxiety and a sense of failure and she did her best to tune out Brett's incessant complaining.

"I'm going out there and make sure those law officers don't make off with something else," Brett said, starting toward the door.

Rebecca stepped in front of the door, her gaze level. All talking stopped as everyone turned their attention to the confrontation.

"Stay in here and sit down, Brett," Rebecca said calmly.

"You're not my boss."

"That's where you're wrong. I am your boss and I can fire you. And I will. On the spot. I realize that Marcus hired you, but he gave me the power to do whatever I feel necessary to make this project happen. And I'll let you go, if you don't do exactly as you've been asked. The last thing Dru and his men need is you tromping around out there. If we have a chance of catching who- ever stole the artifact, we have to let the professionals do their job." She turned and let her gaze fall on everyone in the room. "Dru isn't accusing any of us of theft. He's merely doing his job."

"Hogwash!" Brett said. "I'm not certain he knows how to do his job."

Rebecca bit back a harsh reply, but she couldn't stop herself from pointing out the obvious. "Brett, the artifact was in your care when it was stolen. If you'd been doing your job, we wouldn't be here now."

Anger rose in his eyes before he glanced down. With- out another word he returned to his seat by the fire.

"This will all be over soon, and let's just hope Dru and his men find some indication of who took the arti- fact. If we don't recover it, I'm afraid this is only going to be the beginning of a lot of law-enforcement officials on the premises. I expect full cooperation from everyone here. Is that understood?"

She shifted her gaze from one to the next, wait- ing until she had a nod or a verbal agreement. "Good. Coffee's ready," she said, motioning everyone to get a cup.

"Ms. Barrett." Winston West stepped forward. "Could I ask a question?"

"Sure," she said.

"What the hell is going on here?"

Though the question was asked with a long, lazy drawl, Rebecca tensed. "Someone has stolen an artifact," she said.

"I know that," Winston pressed. "But it's not that simple and you know it. This place has a history."

There was a rumble of assent from some of the other workers.

"A woman was killed here only a few months ago. There're stories all over town about ghosts and hangings and buried treasure and such. And there is some maniac running around playing tape recordings of babies. This is just a little too macabre for me."

"That's right," another of the men said. "I came here to excavate a dig, not get caught up in some past thing that's way too weird."

"There are other jobs in cooler climates," another of the diggers said.

"Hold on," Regina stepped forward. "This isn't Rebecca's fault. These are circumstances beyond her control, and I can tell you right now that my daddy's construction crew won't be run off by a little trouble."

"Thank you, Regina," Rebecca said. "It's true Blackthorn has a troubled past, but that has nothing to do with the present. Or the future. We've had a burglary. I'm sure this isn't the first such thing to happen on a dig where valuable artifacts are found. Let's not let our imaginations and town gossip run away with us. We're all grown-ups, aren't we?" She knew the last would be a challenge to the men, and she was right. The last thing she needed was for the entire archaeological crew to quit.

There was a light tap on the door and one of the deputies stepped inside. "We'd like to talk to the crew, one by one," he said.

"I'll be glad to talk." Winston stepped forward and walked out with the deputy.

Looking around the room at the unhappy faces, Rebecca could only hope that the others would be as cooperative.

DRU STEPPED on the porch and hesitated. It was three in the morning and he didn't want to wake Rebecca if by some miracle she'd fallen asleep. He started to leave, but the door opened a crack and he heard her voice, and it sounded wide-awake.

"I thought I'd give you my initial report," he said.

He heard the chain lock sliding, and the door opened wider. "Come in," she said.

"Let's take a seat out here on the porch," he suggested, easing into a rocker. He was bone tired and discouraged.

Rebecca slipped into the chair beside him and in a moment he felt her fingers curl around his hand.

"Thank you for everything," she said, squeezing his fingers.

His reaction was a jolt of desire that caught him

completely unprepared. A split second before, he'd been too tired to think straight. Now he felt as if electricity had been injected into his body.

"I wish I had more to tell you," he said, his own fingers curling around hers and holding on lightly. "We didn't find any useful physical evidence."

"So the artifact is gone?"

He tightened his grip on her fingers. "Maybe not. That's one item that won't be as easy to sell as jewelry or silver or appliances. As soon as I get back to the office, I'll alert all the antique dealers in the area. If the thief does try to sell it, we'll stand a good chance of catching him then and recovering the bowl."

"That's good."

His eyes had adjusted to the darkness, and he could see that Rebecca was deflated by his news. It did sound like a long shot, even to him. "All of the testimony of the crew seemed to check out."

"That's a relief," Rebecca said, and there was humor in her voice.

"And you have an obvious fan in Regina Batson. I think she wants to grow up to be you," Dru said.

"She is grown," Rebecca pointed out. "Grown and quite self-possessed for a twenty-one-year-old."

"She is that," Dru agreed. "I guess that kind of self-confidence is easy when you've had lots of opportunity."

"You sound as if you know a lot about Regina."

"Not her personally. I've known her family all my life. Eugene and Roy were legends in high school. Of course they'd long graduated by the time I got there. They were brilliant students and won scholarships to the best schools. Eugene in architecture and Roy in mechanical engineering. They make an impressive team. I think everyone was a little surprised when Eugene came home and married Millie, his high-school sweetheart. Some folks considered her from the wrong side of the tracks, and she was a little on the wild side. Or at least she gave that appearance. You know, miniskirts, smoking a little dope, that kind of thing. It was that era."

"Is Regina an only child?"

"Yes, and spoiled rotten as a youngster. I'm glad to see she's grown out of being the self-centered little brat. When she was about twelve, she and a bunch of teenagers got into a little trouble. I remember my dad had a long talk with them." Dru chuckled. "Dad was good with young people. He believed that most kids got into trouble because they wanted parental attention."

"And what do you believe?" Rebecca asked.

"That's true in a lot of cases, but not always." He could hear his voice tightening, but he couldn't stop it. "Some kids get in trouble because they like it. Some kids are just bad."

"Which is one of the reasons you didn't want to have kids?" Rebecca asked.

He was surprised at her astuteness. In his work in law enforcement he'd seen kids from the finest families bring nothing but woe and sorrow to the people who loved them. But his experience with that kind of thing was a little more personal.

"It would seem to be a real crapshoot," he said. "Whether it's genetics or environment, I just haven't been interested in taking the gamble." He rose from his chair. "I have to finish some paperwork at the office, Rebecca. I'll be in touch tomorrow."

As he walked to his car, he chewed over the conversation with Rebecca. She'd never know how close she'd come to stumbling into the emotional quicksand of his life. Everyone in Natchez knew he had a brother, but no one talked about Freddy Colson. No one dared.

REBECCA STRETCHED out in her bed, knowing that dawn wasn't far away. She tried to put the recent events in perspective, but she kept going back to the stolen bowl. This was something she was going to have to report to Aurelia and Marcus. If she could find them. As much as she didn't want to worry them, she was going to have to.

She checked the time and realized it would be midmorning in Spain. There was no time like the present. As she was about to dial a villa where they might be staying, she hesitated. Maybe she could recover the bowl. Why worry Marcus and Aurelia before she gave Dru a chance to apprehend the culprit and recover the stolen item? She replaced the phone and paced the small cottage. It wasn't in her nature to turn over a problem to someone else. She'd been hired to take care of things. She had to at least make an attempt.

She made another pot of coffee and took a cup out onto the porch. Dawn was breaking in the eastern sky.

From the vantage point of the new construction, she'd be able to see the river washed in the pinks and golds of first light. She refilled her coffee cup and walked up the drive.

Passing the encampment where the archaeological crew slept, she considered each of the employees. They were all seasoned excavators, handpicked by Brett.

Brett Gibson had come with the job. Marcus and Aurelia had hired him, but how much did they really know about him? Yes, he was well-respected in his field, but what did that mean? When she returned to the cottage, she intended to find out everything she could about every single person who worked on Blackthorn property.

She heard the sound of a vehicle behind her and turned around to face Eugene Batson. He smiled at her through the window, unaware of the things that had happened during the night.

"Where's my daughter?" he asked.

"Asleep, I hope," Rebecca said. She filled him in on the artifact theft. "Please don't repeat this, but you have a right to know since Regina is working here," she told him.

"It might be best if she comes home at night for a few days."

"That's up to you."

"She has real talent in architecture. Who would have imagined that she'd develop such a passion for digging in the dirt," Eugene said.

"Brett certainly seems to thrive on it."

"I'm wondering if Regina likes the work or the man in charge," Eugene said, and there was a worried note in his voice.

Rebecca wasn't going to weigh in on that subject. Of course Regina was taken with Brett. She'd been on site ever since he arrived. And she was always at his side. Rebecca smiled. "Brett's pretty prickly. Regina must have a tolerant nature."

"No, she's just young," Eugene said. "But I'll have a word with her."

"Mr. Batson, you've lived in Natchez your whole life, do you like Dru Colson?"

Eugene's smile was conspiratorial. "Checking up on your beau?" he asked.

When Rebecca blushed, he shook his head. "I'm sorry. I was only teasing you a little. Dru's a good man. He has a tough job and folks still like him."

"How did you know I was…seeing him?" Rebecca asked.

Eugene laughed out loud. "Nothing goes unnoticed in Natchez. You two were seen dancing. That's as good as an engagement in these parts."

"That's ridiculous."

"Perhaps," he said, still chuckling. "But if you want the scoop on your personal life, you should have breakfast today at Ella's Café. Ella will be able to tell you everything that's been said about you since you took over the job at Blackthorn."

"Maybe that's something I need to hear," Rebecca said as she poured out the remains of her cold coffee.

## CHAPTER SIX

DRU SAT IN HIS personal car in the parking lot and waited for Randall Levert to show up for work. Looking around, Dru took in the changes in the once-thriving used-car business. In the past several months, the car lot had gone downhill. Weeds grew rampant around the building and litter blew between the lines of parked automobiles on the early-morning breeze. The appearance of the lot substantiated what Dru had heard over coffee at Ella's Café—every one of Randall's employees had quit. Not because Randall had been in trouble with the law, but because he'd become unreasonable. Since his release from jail, Randall had become belligerent and abusive to his employees. Or at least that was the gossip in town, being heavily advanced by his former employees.

Vince Eubanks, Randall's head mechanic, had come right out and said that Randall had gone off the deep end.

"He's mad as a hatter," Vince had told Ella and a counter full of other patrons including Dru. "He was always intense. You know, driven to be the best salesman, to turn the most cars, to make the most deals. Now he doesn't care about selling cars or his employees. All he does is sit in his office and stare out the window. He gave everybody bad paychecks. They bounced like a rubber ball at the bank. When we confronted him, he didn't even bat an eye. He just went into his office and closed the door."

Dru had to admit that he was troubled by that description of Randall. Randall had built his business up from the ground. He'd started out selling a car or two off a service station parking lot and gradually became one of the biggest used car dealerships in the Southeast. Randall had never been a popular man, but he'd been a well-respected businessman. But now Randall was throwing everything away. It was as if he didn't care anymore about his business. And a man who'd stepped over the edge was dangerous because he'd already lost everything of importance to him.

Dru finished the cup of coffee he'd gotten at Ella's and drummed his fingers on the steering wheel. At last a black Tahoe pulled in beside the building. Randall got out, and Dru was further shocked by the change in the man's appearance. He'd gone from being a robust, healthy man to an unkempt figure. Dru slowly got out of his car and crossed the parking lot.

Pausing at the door of the showroom, Randall seemed not to recognize Dru. He stared blankly at the sheriff and his forehead furrowed in concentration as if he were trying to place who Dru was.

"I'd like to talk to you, Randall," Dru said easily.

"Go away." Randall turned back to opening the door.

"I want to talk to you and I don't want to have to get a court order to do it," Dru said.

"I have a business to run," Randall flared, and for a moment, Dru thought he sounded like his old self. Impatient and rude, but focused on his car dealership.

"This won't take but a minute and I don't see any customers waiting in line."

"What is it?" Randall didn't wait for Dru to answer. He unlocked the side door of the building and walked inside, leaving Dru to follow or not.

Dru stepped into the building, glad for the air conditioning even though it was still mid May. "Everyone quit," Randall said. "They were only in it for the money. When I couldn't pay them, they all quit. Just like that."

Dru stepped closer so he could get a good look in Randall's eyes. The man seemed genuinely offended that his employees expected to get paid. "Most folks work for a paycheck," Dru offered.

"There were plenty of times I gave them all paychecks when they didn't earn them." Randall glanced at a stack of mail, dropped it back on the empty receptionist's desk and went into his own office. Dru followed. He'd wanted to get a look at Randall's office. And he also wanted to search his house. But that would take more time and a search warrant. Right now he'd have to settle for what he could get from Randall in a "conversation."

"What do you want?" Randall asked, suddenly wary.

"Have you been on Blackthorn property?" Dru asked.

"Of course not. I'll go to prison if I go out to Blackthorn. Besides, Marcus and his wife are gone. They're in Europe. They found the treasure."

"Yes, I know," Dru said. "But someone has been playing tape recordings of a crying baby." He watched closely for Randall's reaction, which was more than he expected.

"Who? Who's doing that?" Randall asked. He stepped closer. "They're doing it so people will think it's me." He grinned. "You thought it was me, didn't you?"

"It crossed my mind," Dru said, wondering how mentally disturbed Randall really might be. "But you're too smart to go on Blackthorn, aren't you?"

"I'm too smart to get sent back to prison," Randall said.

"Where were you last night?" Dru asked.

"At home."

"Alone?"

"Natchez doesn't offer a large social life for a man who was put in prison for the murder of his own mother. I'd have to say that I've been crossed off the better guest lists."

Randall might be off-center, but he was still very smart and aware of what he was doing and saying, Dru realized. "So you were alone?"

"Yes, Sheriff Colson, I was alone. No one to give me an alibi, if I should need one. What happened at Blackthorn?"

"How did you know something happened at Blackthorn?" Dru countered.

"It stands to reason. You say someone's playing games at Blackthorn and then you ask me where I was last night. Easy conclusion that something happened at Blackthorn last night."

"Would you give me permission to search your office here, your vehicle, and your home?"

Randall hesitated. "Why should I?"

"In the interest of the law," Dru said. "If you have nothing to hide, why shouldn't you?"

"It depends on what you're looking for."

Dru considered for a moment. "Did you know Joey Reynolds was living out at Blackthorn?"

"I heard the new lords of Blackthorn built him an apartment of his own. Joey's loyalty to Aurelia was rewarded. Good for him. I hope he enjoys it in good health."

Dru was instantly alert, but he managed not to show his keen interest. "Is there something you know about Joey's health?"

"Only that he's been known to show up in places that generally aren't considered healthy."

There was a definite edge to Randall's voice. "It was Joey who found your cufflink beside your mother's body," Dru said.

"I haven't forgotten that," Randall said, his voice becoming almost singsong. "But Joey only found it. Yvonne put it there."

"Yes," Dru agreed. "So there's no reason for you to hold a grudge against Joey, is there?"

Randall smiled. "I don't hold grudges," he said. "That

would be a waste of time and probably get me into a lot of trouble. I've had enough trouble in my life, Sheriff. Now I have work to attend to. I'd like you to leave."

Dru had no choice. He didn't have enough evidence to arrest Randall, and though he had a lot of additional questions, he knew Randall wasn't going to cooperate. Randall was done with answering questions.

"I'll be back later on," Dru said. "There are several things that don't add up."

"Perhaps you just don't know how to do totals," Randall said, his smile very amused.

"Stay away from Blackthorn, Randall."

"When they finish the house, do you think Ms. Barrett would let me see it?"

It was the oddest request. "Why would you want to?"

"Marcus McNeese wasn't the only person in town who had fantasies about what Blackthorn once was and could be. Call it morbid curiosity, but I'd just like to see the finished product. I hear it's going to be a real showplace. Unique."

"That's what I've been told." Dru couldn't help but be a little curious. If Randall had been on the property, he could easily have seen the new building.

"Ask if I can come and look," Randall pressed.

"That's months down the road. Marcus and Aurelia will be back long before then and you can take the issue up with them yourself. Just make sure you stay off the property until you have their permission."

"You got it, Sheriff." Randall gave a mock salute. "Say, you wouldn't be interested in a car, would you?"

REBECCA TOOK a seat at the counter, smiling as Ella put a cup of hot coffee in front of her without even asking.

"You look a little peaked this morning," Ella commented. "Must be hard work supervising all that's going on at Blackthorn."

"I'm a little tired." Rebecca had come to gather information, not blurt out her business. She wasn't surprised that Ella Jensen recognized her. Before she'd left, Aurelia had taken her into the café for lunch and an introduction to Ella. Aurelia had made it clear that Ella was a good friend to have.

"Dru was in earlier," Ella said. "He looked bushed, too, but his lips were sealed tight. I don't suppose you'd care to tell me what's going on?"

Rebecca sipped the coffee and shook her head. "It would probably be best if I just followed Dru's lead."

Ella smiled. "I heard you did that quite well on the dance floor the other night." She leaned closer. "There are a lot of women in this town who would love to get the chance."

"Dru's a handsome man."

"He's a good man," Ella pointed out. "Handsome men are a dime a dozen. And good looks can hide a lot of ugliness. Dru's good through and through."

Rebecca couldn't help smiling. "Where do I apply for membership to his fan club?"

Ella laughed. "I guess I did get a little carried away."

"Let's just say when Dru runs for sheriff again, I'll expect to see his campaign headquarters right here."

"That's an idea." Ella took her breakfast order and turned it in. She made the rounds of the full tables with her coffeepot, refilling cups and chatting with customers, and then she was back. She picked up Rebecca's breakfast order from the window and placed it in front of her.

"Ella, have you heard anything about Blackthorn lately?" Rebecca asked. It was a blunt way to get into the conversation, but directness seemed the best approach.

"Sure. There's not a day goes by that I don't hear something about Blackthorn. That's just the nature of the place. It's legendary in the town, and I don't think that's going to change for a long, long time."

Rebecca nodded. "Would you tell me exactly what you've heard?" She met Ella's clear gaze.

"Gossip is that someone's been prowling the premises playing tape recordings of crying babies."

"That much is true, but please don't confirm the rumors."

"Folks around here heard so many stories about the ghost of Andre Agee that they're reluctant to believe that it was Marcus dressing up as the ghost. You know people. They like a delicious little thrill. The ghost business is harmless and lends an air of the supernatural to a place that is already bigger than life." Ella leaned closer. "This crying-baby business, though, is just creepy."

"You can say that again. Even though I know it's a tape recording, it sends chills all over me."

"I can't believe they let that skunk Randall Levert walk out of jail. He didn't kill his mother, but he was guilty of trying to frighten Aurelia half to death."

"Tell me about Randall," Rebecca said.

"I've known him most of his life," Ella said. "As a young kid, he seemed just fine. But his mother was a strange bird, and I guess she finally got to him. When he was about twelve he changed. Abruptly. Went from an outgoing, friendly kid to this shy, withdrawn boy who stuttered and stayed home. It was sort of pitiful to see."

"I wonder what happened?"

"It was back in the seventies. That was a strange summer. Old Lionel Agee had the annual summer picnic up on the grounds of Blackthorn, but it was the last one. He announced he was moving to Europe the next day, and he did just that. And then those young folks moved into the woods at Blackthorn and set up what passed for a commune."

"No one tried to stop them?"

"Well, there were several vigilante groups in town who talked big about going up and breaking up 'that communist nest.'" She laughed. "Old George Welsh was sheriff then, and he made a stab at catching the kids with dope, but he could never actually catch them."

"What was the real objection?"

Ella gave Rebecca a puzzled look. "I suppose you're too young to remember that time, but a lot of older folk were badly frightened of what they saw as the coming destruction of society. Young men and women living together in tents, smoking dope, playing guitars, it was just more than decent folk could take."

Rebecca smiled with Ella. "It sounds pretty harmless."

"And it was. But it was different. It was a sign that the world was changing, and change is hard, especially in a small town. Those kids were strangers, and they acted as if they had a right to camp where they pleased. More than anything it was a clash of values."

"And then there was the baby," Rebecca said. She felt a wave of sadness.

"Yes, there was the baby. Of course, George Welsh didn't find it until the young folks were all gone."

"No one ever found who it belonged to?"

"There wasn't DNA and all that stuff back then. The young people had scattered. No one even really knew their names. So the town got together and paid for a funeral for the baby."

"And no attempt was made to prosecute any of the campers for the death of the baby?" Rebecca found it a little hard to accept. "Surely there was some criminal liability. At least neglect."

Ella shook her head. "To be honest, I never heard what the baby died of. Maybe it was born dead. But you could ask Dru. It was Deputy Lance Mullins who found the baby." She pursed her lips. "You know, Lance was Randall's uncle. Isn't that interesting? I never put all of that together, but there is a connection between Randall and Blackthorn that goes beyond his quest for the buried treasure."

"One more question," Rebecca said, realizing that she was monopolizing Ella's time.

"Shoot."

"What are people saying about me?"

"Only that you're too pretty to be so smart."

Rebecca couldn't stop the flush that crept up her neck. "That's ridiculous."

"You asked."

"I've hardly been in town except to buy some supplies."

"It was enough to make an impression. And that dancing business with Dru…" Ella waved her hand. "I heard that was pretty hot."

"Really." Rebecca knew the flush was intensifying.

"There was a table full of young women in here just the other day talking about how they'd like to run you out of town. They weren't real keen on outside competition for Dru's affections."

"He said he wasn't seeing anyone."

"No, he and Celeste broke up a while back. But that doesn't mean she's given up on him. She's a nice young woman, but she was a fool to try and pressure Dru. I think she realizes it now and regrets it."

Rebecca wasn't prepared for the ripple of anxiety that shot through her. "I'm sure Dru would be interested in hearing that."

"Maybe. Maybe not. Dru's a lot like his daddy. He doesn't cover the same ground twice."

Rebecca realized Ella was trying to make her feel better. Her feelings were obviously all over her face. So, she was interested in the sheriff and now everyone in town would know about it.

"What Dru chooses to do is his own business."

"And yours," Ella said. "That's plain enough to see."

Instead of denying it, Rebecca took a deep breath. "What do folks think about the dig going on at the Indian burial mound?"

"Some folks think there's more treasure buried there." She laughed. "There's always going to be that aspect of Blackthorn to contend with. But most folks are glad that something is being done to document the past and preserve it. A lot of Mississippi history was lost because no one thought to record the history of the original inhabitants. But be warned, Rebecca. That man, Brett Gibson, needs some lessons in tact and diplomacy. Everywhere he goes he annoys people."

"That seems to be Brett's special gift," Rebecca said with a sigh.

"Keep him on a short leash and whenever possible, send someone else into town. He isn't well liked."

"I think Regina Batson has a crush on him," Rebecca said. "She's in for a rocky summer." She found it incredibly easy to talk with Ella. It was as though they'd been friends forever.

"Might do her good," Ella said. "She's been the little town princess since she could toddle."

"Dru said she was spoiled."

"That's a mild term for it. But she's a smart girl. A little exposure to someone who won't kiss her feet might be just the ticket for her."

"That's a job Brett can handle with his hands tied behind his back."

Rebecca stood up.

"I asked the cook to make something for Joey. If you're headed back to Blackthorn would you take him these blueberry pancakes? They're his favorite."

"I'd be delighted to."

## CHAPTER SEVEN

DRU WAS SURPRISED when he found John Ittawasa waiting in his office for him, but almost instantly he realized he shouldn't have been. John had an uncanny ability to sense what was going on. And Dru could see by his face that he was well aware of the theft of the artifact—and very angry about it.

"I want to post security at Blackthorn. I want some men I trust there at all times," John said without preamble. "A valuable piece of history has been stolen."

Dru motioned him into a chair and walked over to close his office door. It was almost impossible to keep rumors down in Natchez but there was no point feeding the gossip more than could be helped.

"How'd you hear about the theft?"

John shrugged. "It doesn't matter."

"It could," Dru said. "As far as I know the only people who know about the theft are the people at Blackthorn and the thief. It doesn't make sense to me that the Blackthorn employees are blabbing about their own lack of security."

"Roy Batson called me."

"Damn! The contractors," Dru added, sighing.

"Regina was right in the middle of it. I'm sure she told her uncle and her father."

"Have you found any leads as to who stole the bowl?" John asked.

"Nothing conclusive."

"I urged Mr. Gibson to take the proper precautions. He's an arrogant man who puts his ego and ambition ahead of his responsibility. Had he listened to me, that bowl would have been well secured."

"Gibson is hard to take," Dru agreed, "but he does seem to be a professional. Aurelia and Marcus went through an extensive search for just the right archaeologist before they settled on him."

"They made a mistake. He's incompetent."

Dru realized that the dislike between John and Brett went a lot deeper than he'd first thought. Normally John wasn't an emotional man. He could put his personal feelings on the back burner. Not so with Brett.

"Brett isn't in charge of Blackthorn. Rebecca Barrett is. You should take your ideas on security up with her."

"I will," John said, "but first tell me what you discovered."

Dru liked John Ittawasa, but like only went so far. He wasn't obliged to report to him. "Why don't you tell me what you know," Dru said.

"Only that the bowl was in Brett's tent. There was some confusion about someone running around on the property, and the bowl was taken." John's stare was direct. "I thought the ghosts of Blackthorn had all been cleared out."

Dru nodded. "Whoever is on the property, it isn't a ghost. Any idea who might be running around up there?"

John's smile was amused. "No."

"That's good, John, because even though I'm sympathetic to your cause, I would be really unhappy if I discovered that you were trying to use the past to your advantage here."

"I understand perfectly, and I assure you that no one from my organization has been on Blackthorn soil."

"Good."

"But I'm going there now. If there are additional finds, they'll be taken into the custody of the Choctaw nation and put in a safe place."

"Work it out with Ms. Barrett. But stay away from Brett Gibson," Dru said, picking up his coat as he prepared to follow John to Blackthorn. The last thing he needed was a confrontation between John and Brett.

IT DID REBECCA good to see Joey almost attack the blueberry pancakes that Ella had sent him.

"I'll be glad to share with you," Joey said as he drizzled even more syrup on his plate.

"You go right ahead." Rebecca went to the refrigerator and poured him a glass of milk. "How are you feeling, Joey?"

"Okay." He rubbed the knot on his head. "It's going away."

"Joey, has Randall Levert said anything to you lately?"

Joey slowly lowered his fork. "In the courtroom. He said he was going to get even with me." He fidgeted with his napkin. "He was angry and he was upset about his mother."

"Are you afraid of Randall?"

Joey thought about it for a moment. "No."

"That's good." She was relieved, but she was also curious. "Why not?"

"He always talks big. He's always saying things he doesn't do. He's always done it. Like at the church one time I dropped some coffee on his shoe and he got mad and said I was going to have to buy him a new pair. But he never made me." Joey picked up his fork again. "I feel sorry for Randall."

"You do? Why?"

"He always seems…like he has to pretend. His mama was mean to him, and so was his uncle. One time, when he and his uncle were hunting at Blackthorn and I was living with my mama there, I heard someone yelling. It was Randall. His uncle was hitting him."

"His uncle was a deputy."

"Yeah. Everyone called him Stick because he was always hitting his hand with his nightstick. He was mean."

"And he's dead?"

Joey shrugged. His appetite had returned and he pushed a big forkful of pancake into his mouth.

Rebecca refilled his milk glass. "Stay away from Brett today, okay?"

Joey's mouth was so full he couldn't answer, so he nodded.

"Brett's looking for someone to blame for his screw-up. The simplest thing for you is just to stay away from the dig site."

Joey nodded again, making a circle with his thumb and finger to show he fully understood.

Rebecca was still smiling when she walked through the stables to make sure the horses had water. Cogar was due for a ride, but he would have to wait. She started back to the construction site. The crew was scheduled to begin stacking the blocks to finish off the first floor of the house. It was going to be exciting watching the walls go up almost as if by magic.

In her opinion, Marcus and Aurelia had made a perfect choice in the concrete-block design. The house would stand for centuries.

She was passing by the old homesite when she stopped to glance at the columns that stood as silent reminders of the past. She was glad that Marcus and Aurelia had decided on putting their new home at a different location. Modern building techniques and materials had allowed them to set their house site right on the bluff. The columns would be preserved, a reminder of a man and a lifestyle gone but not forgotten.

She was about to move on when she heard raised voices. Brett's was easy to recognize. She was used to hearing the man yell. She didn't recognize the second voice, but it, too, was tense with anger.

She hurried to the dig site and stopped short when she saw Dru standing between Brett and John Ittawasa. She cursed the grapevine that seemed to run from Blackthorn all over southeast Mississippi. How had Ittawasa found out about the stolen artifact so quickly? It didn't matter now. She'd hoped to tell John about the burglary herself. Now she'd just have to deal with the fallout.

"Brett!" she called as she hurried up the steps that had been built into the side of the burial mound. "Brett!"

"It's okay," Dru reassured her as she arrived, breathless, at the top.

"It's a damn sight from being okay," Brett raged. "I won't have anyone sitting over me like a baby-sitter."

"You lost the privilege of being treated as a grown-up when you lost the artifact," John Ittawasa said.

"Hey, easy!" Rebecca said, stepping so close to Dru that she could feel the heat of his body. She put her hands out, one toward John and the other to Brett. "Let's get off the top of this hot mound and talk about this in some shade." She was squinting against the glare of the sun and far away, down the bluff, the Mississippi glittered.

"I won't have this man treating me like I don't know my job," Brett said, his words barely able to escape his clenched jaw.

"Not another word," Rebecca said harshly. "Everyone! Off the burial mound. Now. We'll settle this like professionals, not a bunch of sandlot kids."

Winston crawled out of the hole he'd been digging. "I could use a break," he said agreeably. "Come on, guys. There's some iced tea down at the campsite."

"My mother sent some cookies," Regina added, wiping the sweat from her brow with the back of her hand. She stood only a few feet from Brett and her gaze was riveted on him. "A break is a good idea."

The men started off the mound, chatting among themselves and Rebecca silently blessed Winston and Regina for their good sense. Brett had no choice but to follow his crew. Dru went after Brett and she held John Ittawasa's stare until he, too, started off the mound. She followed last, aware that her heart was pounding and her head throbbed. There were always headaches associated with a big project, but she'd never worked with a more volatile man than Brett Gibson. Perhaps hiring him, no matter how good his credentials, had been a mistake.

The crew went to their campsite but Rebecca led John, Brett and Dru to her cottage. Tempers would be cooler in the air-conditioning. She poured cold drinks for everyone before they began. She gave each man a chance to have his say before she made her decision.

"Brett, don't take this the wrong way, but I think Mr. Ittawasa has a real point. There is someone on this property. Perhaps it was a deliberate diversion so that the artifact could be stolen. If John is willing to loan us some men to help with security, I think we'd be foolish to turn down that help."

"But I don't want outsiders—"

She cut him short. "We all have a vested interest in

what you discover. This dig is bigger than you or me. It belongs to a lot of people. We're going to accept John's help and be glad of it."

"Not at the dig site. Let them guard the perimeter." Brett's eyes flashed a warning.

"This may be a really good decision," Dru said. "I can't post deputies up here, but I'll feel a lot better with some additional security. John's men are well trained."

"And as soon as we find anything of value, someone will take it immediately to the vault at the bank," Rebecca continued. "That will serve two purposes. The artifacts will be safe and everyone in town will know that the valuable things are not kept on site. That should cut down on potential robberies."

Dru had withdrawn and stood at the kitchen sink, stepping out of the situation as much as possible. Rebecca appreciated that. He was a man who didn't feel the need to express his opinion, but she could clearly see that he was behind her. When he caught her eye, he gave her a warm smile.

"Where will these security men be posted?" Brett asked in a growl.

"Two will patrol the perimeter of Blackthorn with road access," John said carefully, "and one will stay at the entrance."

Rebecca touched John's arm in gratitude. He'd won the battle, but he was going to be gracious. He hadn't insisted on putting a man at the dig site.

"We appreciate your assistance, Mr. Ittawasa," she

said. "Now I think I'd like to go over the description of the stolen bowl with you so that we can do our best to retrieve it. Luckily, we documented the find with Polaroid snapshots, and we have some very clear views of the bowl."

"I've alerted all the antique dealers in the region," Dru said. "If the thief tries to fence it, we stand a good chance of getting it returned to us."

John nodded. "We'll all work together on this."

"I have work to do." Brett put his untouched tea down on the table and stalked out of the cabin. Rebecca let him go. He was incapable of grace or courtesy. It was too bad. In the long run, he was the only person who'd suffer from his bad attitude.

AN HOUR LATER, Dru was finished at Blackthorn. All in all, things had gone much better than he'd expected. And he was relieved that there was going to be additional security at the estate. John had promised that his men would be at Blackthorn in the morning.

Without telling anyone but Rebecca, Dru had posted a deputy at the landing on the riverbank. If the intruder attempted to tie up there again, he'd be apprehended.

He was about to drive away when he caught sight of Rebecca coming down the drive on a big gray horse. She was a sight, the sun sparkling in her hair and her face alive with pleasure. The size of the horse made her look small, and the riding pants and boots set off her slender legs and trim waist. After five minutes, he realized that he could watch her for hours and never grow tired, she sat on the horse with such grace and confidence.

"I thought you'd gone back to town," Rebecca said as she walked the horse up beside his vehicle. He hoped it was pleasure that he saw in her face. The truth was that he'd delayed finishing up with John, hoping that he would see her again.

"I was just tying up some loose ends up with John. The men he sends will be good, Rebecca. I have to tell you I'm relieved."

"Me, too. All in all, it's going to be a good thing. As soon as I get a chance, I'm going to Ella's to spread the word."

Dru laughed. "So, you've discovered that Ella's is the heartbeat of the town."

"That and gossip central."

"Yes, I gather you know that you've been the topic of a lot of that talk." He grinned. "I've heard a number of things about you. I think I may have to bring you in for an interrogation."

"Ah, my dark past has been unearthed," she said, laughing.

"I've heard talk that you cast spells on men." The sun was warm on Dru's arm in the car window. Once again, he was so keenly aware of the small pleasures of the day. In Rebecca's presence, everything gained intensity.

"Yes, so I heard this morning. I hear there's a hit team of ladies gunning for me. It seems I'm the hussy who's stalking the town's most eligible bachelor."

Dru laughed. "Don't believe everything you hear. I've

been single a long time and haven't noticed that much interest from the town ladies."

Rebecca rolled her eyes. "Would you have noticed? Men are notoriously obtuse about some things."

He could see that she was having a good time teasing him, and he felt a strange warmth spread through his chest. With everything going on at Blackthorn, Rebecca could still find a smile and a few minutes to quip and tease. He liked that about her.

"How about we stir up the town talk again tonight? There's this great little bar that serves the best catfish. La Belle's. They also have a Cajun band that will make your feet itch to get on the dance floor."

"I don't think your reputation can stand more dancing with me," Rebecca said. "I hear dancing is like a public declaration of marriage here in Natchez."

Dru lifted his sunglasses. "I've never been one to worry about gossip. Let's have some fun."

"You're the one who has to live here—and run for re-election," Rebecca teased.

"I'm willing to risk it."

"Then dinner and dancing sounds fun. What time?"

"Eight o'clock. The band doesn't really get cranked up until about ten."

"What, exactly, does one wear for Cajun dancing?"

"Anything one finds comfortable," Dru said. He started the car and slowly drove away, his gaze lingering on her in the rearview mirror as she put the big horse into a trot.

# CHAPTER EIGHT

REBECCA SANK DOWN in her chair, breathless. "That's the fastest waltz I've ever danced," she said, laughing at Dru's obvious delight.

"No one ever said a waltz had to be sedate."

"Your point is proven." Rebecca sipped her drink. She couldn't stuff another bite of food down. She'd eaten catfish, fried onion rings, fried dill pickles, slaw and hush puppies. Now the only thing that could save her would be a lot more dancing. She was about to suggest a two-step when she saw something that stopped her in her tracks. Brett and his entire crew were seating themselves at the bar.

"They left Blackthorn unattended," she said, rising to her feet. She didn't wait for a response from Dru but walked over to the men. "Brett, can I speak with you?" she asked. When he didn't respond, she felt anger wash over her. "You left the dig site unattended!"

Brett glanced over his shoulder. "Why should my men stay at Blackthorn when John Ittawasa's men are there?"

He knew she was upset and why. His flippant attitude sent a wave of anger over her. "Because that's what you agreed to do—always leave a man on site. Remember?"

"That was before we got the guard dogs."

"John Ittawasa's men don't work for Aurelia. Yours do."

"I'll go back," Winston said, sliding off the barstool. "No problem for me."

"But it is for me," Brett said. "If those Choctaws are such good guards, they don't need us up there."

"That isn't your call to make, it's mine. I want someone on my payroll there at all times. I want someone who's going to be accountable. That was part of the job you signed on to do, Brett."

"I'm outta here," Winston said, sauntering toward the door.

Rebecca knew that it wouldn't do any good to press the matter in a public restaurant, but tomorrow, at Blackthorn, Brett was going to come to terms with his position or he was going to be fired. She'd had more than she could take.

"I hear the sheriff has some mighty fancy footwork," Brett said, a cruel grin illuminating his face. "Regina tells me he's quite the lady's man."

"Maybe he's willing to give some lessons. I'll be sure and ask him on your behalf," Rebecca replied tartly. "Then again, I'm not sure you can afford it. It would take a fortune to teach you a little charm."

"Some women find me charming enough."

Rebecca was about to walk away, but something in Brett's tone made her stop. She studied his face, but she couldn't see anything except his desire to torment her and it was something she didn't understand. There were times when it seemed Brett's anger and ill-humor were reserved especially for her. "What's eating at you, Brett?" She'd rather confront him than pretend nothing was going on.

"Brett!" The door of the restaurant swung closed with a whoosh and Regina almost ran to the bar. "Hi," she said, her gaze lingering on Brett before she finally acknowledged Rebecca. "Hello, Rebecca. What are you doing here?"

"Dining with her beau," Brett snapped.

"There's a great dance band here," Regina said, oblivious to the tension between the two. "Dance with me, Brett. You promised."

His gaze on Rebecca, Brett followed Regina to the dance floor. He turned so that his back faced the bar.

"I'm sorry, Ms. Barrett," Tony said. "We can all go back. None of us really wanted to leave anyway. Brett was just determined that we come to town. He takes things a little too personal, if you know what I mean."

"It's okay," Rebecca said. "Brett is the man I hold responsible for fulfilling his duties. He's the one who signed on for his job. If Winston is at the site, that's enough for me. For tonight."

Dru had ordered another round of drinks when she returned to the table. "I'm so sorry," she said. "Brett just seems to defy me at every turn. And the stupid thing is that he's biting off his nose to spite his face."

"I'd say that's his nature."

"He resents me because I'm a woman," Rebecca said flatly.

"That or else he's attracted to you and hates you because you're with another man."

Rebecca gave Dru a sharp look to see if he was teasing her. When she realized he was serious, she shook her head and nodded toward the dance floor where Brett and Regina were laughing and hollering as they performed a complicated set of steps. "Brett's no fool. Regina Batson is her daddy's little girl. She's beautiful and she's infatuated with him. He could go a long way and do a lot worse."

"You're trying to mix sense and economics into an emotional equation. I'm talking heart. The heart doesn't always follow money, Rebecca."

"Brett has given me nothing but grief even before I started going out with you."

Dru started to say something else but stopped. He lifted his drink and waited for her to raise hers. "To Blackthorn," he said softly.

They touched glasses and drank. Rebecca deliberately avoided looking at the dance floor but she could hear Regina's squeal of laughter as she and Brett continued to dance. Rebecca was ready to leave, but she knew it would be best to wait a little while, just so Brett wouldn't get the idea he'd made her rush back to Blackthorn.

"Would you like anything else, Rebecca?" Dru asked.

What she really wanted was to be alone with Dru. She stared across the table at him, caught again in the strength of his features. His eyebrows were dark, well-formed, his brown hair neatly cut. She'd touched his body a few times and knew it was lean and hard.

His knee brushed her leg beneath the table and she felt a rush so powerful she inhaled sharply. He heard her and understood, and for a moment the electricity between them was so intense it was as if they were grounded in the force of their unspoken feelings, their gazes locked together.

Rebecca was so caught up in the moment that she didn't even see the young woman who walked over to the table and put her hands lightly on Dru's shoulders.

"Hey, Sheriff," she said, giggling, "I thought you might want to arrest me and maybe search me."

Rebecca was so shocked that she simply stared. The young woman was beautiful, a redhead with plenty of cleavage showing and big green eyes.

"Lici," Dru said, shrugging out from under her hands. "What are you doing?"

"We thought you'd joined the priesthood after you and Celeste broke it off, but since you're back in the dating game, I thought I'd tell you I'm interested and available."

Dru's face was flushed. "I'm involved, as you can plainly see."

Lici gave Rebecca an assessing glance. "Yeah, the project manager from Blackthorn. Everyone in town's been talking about her. She may be new, but that doesn't mean she's better than the local girls."

"I think your friends are waiting on you," Dru said,

nodding at the table of young women who were laughing and whooping at Lici's boldness.

"They're all wishing they had the nerve to come over here."

"Lici, I'm not interested."

The green eyes hardened and returned to Rebecca. "She's not that special, Dru."

Dru stood very slowly. There was tension in his body as he stared down at the woman. "Go back to your friends, Lici, and don't bother trying this again. I'm not interested."

"She's going to be bad luck for you, Dru. Mark my words. That woman is going to be nothing but bad luck for you. Everyone in town knows Blackthorn is cursed."

Lici swayed back to her table.

DRU COULDN'T READ the expression on Rebecca's face. She seemed calm, but there was a pulse beating in her neck so strongly that he could see it jump beneath her pale skin.

"Who is she?" Rebecca finally asked.

"Local school teacher."

"What does she teach, sexual aggression?"

Dru laughed, glad that Rebecca could make a joke. "Science, I believe. I also thought she was one of Celeste's friends. I guess I was wrong about that."

He saw Rebecca's expression shift and he looked back at the table of women where Regina now sat. They were all laughing at something Lici was saying. He scouted the bar but didn't see Brett anywhere. When he looked back at the table, Lici gave him a come-hither motion with her hand and Regina burst into laughter.

"I'd like to take a walk around Blackthorn," Dru said.

"You must have been reading my thoughts," Rebecca said as she rose from her chair. She was more than ready to leave.

Dru left money on the table and held Rebecca's elbow as they left. Behind them was a loud burst of feminine laughter and a few catcalls.

"Those ladies play hardball," Rebecca said once they were outside.

"You must be mistaken. Those weren't ladies. I'm curious that Regina was so friendly with them."

"I think she might have aligned herself with Brett, and in her viewpoint that may mean against me," Rebecca said in a rueful tone.

"She's young. That's a kid's mistake."

"Dru, why haven't you dated since you broke up with Celeste?" Rebecca asked as she settled into Dru's car.

He didn't answer until he'd gotten behind the wheel. "The truth is, I was hoping Celeste would make the first move. You know, find someone to date and get on with her life. I didn't want to rub her nose in it. And the second reason is that I hadn't met anyone I wanted to go out with. Until you."

Her smile was warm. "Ah, I almost forgot that the first time I met you I recognized you were a flatterer."

"Only when it's the truth," Dru said. "I'm sorry,

Rebecca. No one in town really cares about my private life, but I think because you're viewed as an outsider, it's caused some sort of bizarre competition."

Rebecca laughed out loud. "That makes sense in a strange kind of way. I guess that means I've been up in the woods at Blackthorn too long if the local logic is beginning to make sense."

"I'm just glad you don't take any of it seriously." He was very glad. In the privacy of the car he felt again the electric jolt at being close to Rebecca. His hand captured hers and his fingers stroked the sensitive flesh of her wrist. She made no effort to withdraw her hand, instead her fingers curled around his, clinging.

The atmosphere in the car was charged, and Dru drove carefully to Blackthorn. As he pulled up in front of the cottage, he wanted to draw Rebecca into his arms and kiss her. They'd been building toward this moment ever since the first time he'd laid eyes on her. Now he didn't want to rush it.

He got out of the car and opened her door, handing her out. As she stepped close to him, he put his arms around her and she melted, her face lifting for his kiss.

Dru had known kissing Rebecca would be magic, but he wasn't prepared for the flood of desire and tenderness that swept over him. She was perfect. She was the woman of his dreams, and he was suddenly terrified that somehow he'd mess it up.

"I can feel your heart racing," Rebecca said, her hand against his chest, pressing.

"I've never wanted a woman like I want you." He could risk nothing less than total honesty.

"I'm on to your sweet talk," Rebecca teased.

"If only it were just flattery," Dru said, and there was a rough edge of his voice. "If we're going to take that walk, we'd better go now or I won't be able to."

Rebecca hesitated. Her hands caught both of his and held on. "Why don't we go inside instead?" she suggested.

He almost couldn't believe her invitation. She wasn't naive. She knew what she was doing. And he wasn't a fool. He didn't have to be asked twice.

REBECCA CLOSED the cottage door and locked it. As she turned the key she knew full well she was locking out the rest of the world. Suddenly nervous, she turned around and saw Dru standing in front of the cold fireplace, staring at her. Heat scorched through her body and she burned for his touch.

Passion was dangerous, though. Its heat seared away reason and reality. In many ways she hardly knew Dru Colson. He'd told her little of his family, and she'd been equally reticent about her own. Somehow, though, it didn't matter. She knew him in a way she'd never known another person.

"I don't want you to regret this or have second thoughts," Dru said, and she knew that he saw her as clearly as she saw him.

"No second thoughts," she said, walking to him and

putting her arms around his neck. "Just a little bit of…
fear." She felt she could be totally honest with him.

"I know." His hands caught at her waist, his fingers
touching her lower back, gently drawing her closer.

She relaxed, putting her concerns aside. Things
wouldn't change between them. They were both grown
and knew exactly what they were getting into. The depth
of emotion she felt for Dru was out of proportion for
the time she'd known him. But life had taught her that
someone as wonderful as Dru didn't come along every
day. There were no guarantees on the future. She could
take the risk or live the rest of her life wondering what
it would have been like.

"Folks say that you only regret the things you've
never done," Dru whispered in her ear.

She kissed his cheek, smiling at the ease with which
he seemed to read her mind. "I won't regret this. It's just
like stepping off a cliff into the unknown, though."

"Everything's fine as long as we step off together,"
he said, taking her hand and leading her into the
bedroom.

DRU MADE COFFEE the next morning and sipped a cup
as he stood at the foot of the bed and watched Rebecca
sleep. She made an art of it, her arms and legs flung over
the bed, her hair tangled and catching the glint of the
sun in golden threads. She was the most beautiful thing
he'd ever seen. And the most generous lover.

He'd begun to fear that he was dreaming and that at

any moment he'd wake up and realize the night before had been only fantasy.

Her eyes opened and she smiled. "Good morning, Sheriff. Is that coffee I smell?"

He got her a cup, remembering that she drank it black, and brought it to the bed. "How are you?"

Her blue gaze held his. "I must be dead," she said with a happy grin. "Surely this can't be a mortal experience. It was too good."

He joined her in laughter. There were times they thought so much alike that it was uncanny. "I should probably get out of here," Dru said. "Your men will be waking up soon, and I'm afraid I've compromised your reputation."

Rebecca shook her head. "My reputation is my business, Dru. Stay and let me make some breakfast. Most of my cooking supplies are up at Joey's, but I have a few things down here."

"Okay," he agreed because just watching her gave him such pleasure.

She was about to get up when there was a knock at the cottage door. Dru already had his pants on so he slipped into his shirt as Rebecca threw on some jeans and a top. She went to the door barefoot, her hand raking through her tangled curls.

"Regina," she said, the surprise so clear in her voice that Dru heard it. "What are you doing here?"

"My mother wanted to look at the burial mound. I wanted to check with you and make sure it was okay before I said she could."

Dru caught the antagonism in Regina's voice and wondered how far the young woman would carry her crush on Brett. It was one thing to be loyal and quite another to be stupid, and Regina was beginning to fall into the latter category.

"I'm sorry, Ms. Barrett, I told Regina this could wait until you got up."

Dru recognized Millie's voice. She'd worked hard on elocution and enunciation, but the back roads still echoed in her tone. Dru had stepped back beside the fireplace with his coffee mug in hand, and he chose to remain there, though he felt Millie's curious gaze on him.

"It's fine, Mrs. Batson. Look around all you'd like. Just stay out of the areas that Brett points out to you."

"I'm very excited about this dig," Millie said, "but I'm a little superstitious. Aren't you afraid this is going to stir up a lot of old ghosts? I mean Blackthorn already has a reputation for being haunted."

"We're hoping that by exploring the burial mound we'll be able to learn more about the history of the Native Americans who lived here first," Rebecca said patiently. "If we don't examine the mound, we won't be able to learn anything."

"Oh, I realize that. It's just a little…ghoulish, isn't it? Sort of like grave robbing?" Millie laughed nervously.

"Mother!" Regina snapped. "Don't be a fool."

"The burial mound is very old," Rebecca said, more kindly. "I guess archaeologists have to weigh the good of learning against the taboo of digging up the dead. In this instance, we have the full backing of the Choctaw people," she pointed out.

"Oh," Millie said. "Are you sure? I heard this morning at Ella's that John Ittawasa has decided that the digging in the mound should be stopped."

## CHAPTER NINE

"I'LL TALK TO John as soon as I get cleaned up," Dru promised. By mutual agreement they'd decided to postpone breakfast until another time.

"I can't believe this is happening," Rebecca said. She was taken aback at the possibility that John had dropped his support of the excavation.

"Then don't. Gossip is rampant in a town this size. John could have made a harmless comment, which was then repeated, changed, repeated again, until it turned into this. Just don't jump to any conclusions."

Rebecca walked up to Dru and gave him a big hug. "Thank you," she said. "Just when I feel the glue coming loose, you say just the right thing to keep me held together."

"Of all the women I've ever met, you're the least likely to come unglued," Dru said, kissing her lips gently. "Rebecca, last night was incredible."

"For me, too." She felt another surge of desire at the memory. With Dru, the intimacy had been magical. They'd made love and talked, holding nothing back. In her relationship with Mike, she'd always felt guarded, as if she had to withhold certain elements of her nature. With Dru all of the boundaries were down.

"I'm sorry we got caught by Millie."

There was such a tone of ruefulness in Dru's voice that Rebecca laughed. "Don't be silly. Had she not come up here it would have been all over town in half an hour anyway. You know that."

"True, but I still hate it."

"Best to get it over with. In fact, you should go straight to Ella's this morning, have some breakfast, and give the details. That way we'll at least start with the straight story."

He gave her a hug. "I love your humor, Rebecca." He stepped back from her, his eyes narrowing. "I should have told you last night. I'm falling in love with you."

Rebecca drank in the words. No more important thing would ever be said to her. "Dru, that means more to me than you'll ever know." She touched his cheek lightly, basking in the light that shone in his eyes. "I feel the same way."

He kissed her forehead, her nose and, finally, her lips. What started as tenderness turned to passion in only seconds.

Laughing softly, he broke the kiss and backed away from her. "I think I'm going to have to go to Ella's and tell the truth. That a woman from Memphis has cast a spell on me. I'm definitely caught in the web you weave."

DRU WASN'T LAUGHING when he finally caught up with John Ittawasa in the chancery clerk's office at the courthouse. John wasn't happy either.

"What's going on?" Dru asked him, both men stepping into the record room for a moment of privacy.

"My men at Blackthorn reported that the site was abandoned last night. Ms. Barrett and all of her employees simply left. There was no guard posted, no attempt made to secure the area from trespassers or thieves. I don't feel that the burial mound or any artifacts are safe."

Dru understood John's concern and told him so. "The truth is, Brett did that deliberately. He's angry about your men being on the property, so he acted a fool. As soon as Rebecca found out about it, she made sure there was someone on the property."

John's mouth softened, but only slightly. "I bear Ms. Barrett no grudge. She has her hands full with that arrogant ass. But my duty is to the mound, the contents and my people. My compassion for Ms. Barrett must come second. I want the dig halted, at least until we can come up with a plan of security that is fail-safe."

"Let's get together with Rebecca this afternoon. Maybe we can work this out without stopping the dig."

For the first time, John smiled. "You're either in love with that woman or you've become a fan of Brett Gibson. I can easily guess which it is."

Dru flushed but his eyes held only delight. "I'm that easy to read?"

"You are," John said. "Arrange the meeting and we'll discuss this with Ms. Barrett."

Dru walked across the hall to his office. He caught the amused glances of the dispatcher and two deputies and realized that Rebecca's predictions were right on the money. Everyone in town already knew he'd spent the night with her, and it was a source of gossip and delight for most of them. But he saw no malice in the smiles that were cast his way. Everyone seemed happy for him, and that made him smile back.

He closed his office door and sat down at his desk, reading over the reports that had been left there by his men. No new physical evidence had been turned up in the theft of the artifact. He went back over the details of the night, remembering the crying baby and the pandemonium. Still, it would be difficult for a thief to have slipped into the heart of the campsite, stolen the bowl and gone without being seen by anyone. The simple conclusion was that the artifact had been stolen by one of the men on Brett's crew. He made a list of all the employees and turned it over to a deputy to run a check on. It might be interesting to see what showed up.

Brett's name was at the top of the list and Dru waited for the results on the dig director. When the computer check came back with no criminal record, he felt both satisfaction and disappointment. It would have been so convenient to discover that Brett was a criminal.

He knew he'd have to go and tell Rebecca about John Ittawasa's concerns, but he found himself reluctant to do so. She had so much on her already. If only he could solve the theft. He'd hardly formed the thought before he found himself chuckling. He was like a school kid. He wanted to impress Rebecca, to come to her rescue like a white knight. Somehow, he'd slipped from reality into a fairy-tale role in a matter of days. And one very incredible night, he reminded himself.

He picked up the phone. So much for fantasies. He had to tell Rebecca about John, and he had to do it fast.

He dialed Blackthorn and waited for an answer. After twelve rings, he decided there was nothing to do but drive up to the site. One thing he intended to mention to Rebecca was the necessity of getting a cell phone. Aurelia had had several bad nights at Blackthorn when the phone lines had been down. A cell phone would alleviate that situation, and it would also give Dru some peace of mind. She'd be able to call for help should she need it.

As he walked across the main office, he called out to the dispatcher that he was headed to Blackthorn. His answer was a long, low wolf whistle.

When he turned around to see who'd whistled, all of the deputies and the dispatcher were busy at their desks, heads down.

Dru couldn't stop the grin that spread across his face. "Is there anything you want to say to me?" Dru asked.

Lyle McKay, one of the deputies, looked up. "No, sir," he said in a deadly serious tone. "But if you have something else to do, I can pick up whatever's happening at Blackthorn."

Lyle had been a deputy for Dru's father, and he'd been a big help in training the young sheriff when the burden of the job fell on Dru. "I think I can handle it," Dru said, equally serious.

"Well, if you need help, we're here to serve."

"Good, just check out that list of names I gave you and find something that can put us on the track of an artifact thief. That would be some really valuable help, instead of cracking wise." There was no sting in Dru's words, just good-natured kidding.

"Let me walk outside with you, son. I may have some advice from an older, wiser and more experienced officer," Lyle said, putting his arm around Dru's shoulders as they walked out together.

Dru was a little surprised. It had been a long time since Lyle had pulled the fatherly routine on him. As soon as they were out in the hallway, Dru gave him a questioning look. "What's up?" he asked.

"There's no easy way to say this," Lyle said and all sense of kidding was gone from his face. "Your brother's back in town."

Dru felt that jolt of emotion that always came with the mention of Freddy. "When did he get here?"

"Apparently he's been here about a week. He called Kitty last night."

Kitty was Lyle's wife. "What did he say?"

"Just that he was in town for a few days."

"Is he in trouble?" Dru asked, dreading the answer.

"He didn't say so, but I suspect he is. Why else would he be back in Natchez? It's the last place he can run to when he's been everywhere else."

"There's nothing here for him," Dru said, his voice cold and bleak.

"Dru, you don't owe him anything."

Dru nodded. "I know that, Lyle. It's just hard to believe it sometimes. And certainly Freddy thinks I owe him a lot. He'll always believe that I got more love, more time, more attention. More of everything than he did. He can never see that he's the one who walked away from it."

"I know," Lyle said. "I remember the past well." He patted Dru's shoulder. "Go on up to Blackthorn and tell that pretty gal how lucky she is to be seeing a man like you."

Dru hesitated. "Did Freddy say where he was staying?"

Lyle shook his head. "No, Kitty asked him, but he didn't say."

Dru could see the deputy was worried and working hard to hide it.

"I'm sure he'll be in touch," Lyle added.

"Yeah, me too."

REBECCA WATCHED the big crane lift the blocks into place, stacking them like giant versions of a child's toy set. It was amazing. The house was taking form minute by minute. The blocks were a lovely shade of hazy gold, stained in the process of mixing the cement. They'd never fade or need painting. A maintenance-free house. The idea was fabulous.

"What do you think?" Roy Batson asked, walking over as he removed his hard hat and wiped the sweat from his forehead.

"I'm impressed," Rebecca said. "It's a fabulous design, Roy. Aurelia and Marcus are going to be knocked on their…behinds by this." She laughed. "If only things at the dig were going this smoothly."

"Regina told me there was a theft," he said. "I made you a list of all my employees." He reached into his back pocket and pulled out a sheet of typewritten paper. "I work only local guys, and most of them I've known for the last two decades. I marked the new ones for you." He showed her two names. "You might ask Dru to check them out."

"Thanks." She was warmed by his cooperation and concern.

"Now I need to ask something of you," he said.

"What can I help you with?"

"It's Regina. Is she safe on the site of the dig? Eugene wants her to go home at night and she's resisting."

Rebecca considered the question and what Roy might be asking. Surely he could see his niece was enamored of Brett Gibson. But Regina was twenty-one. She was old enough to chart her own romantic course. So was Roy asking about physical safety or emotional?

"John Ittawasa is posting some guards around the property. Dru and his officers are working on the theft of the artifact." She gave him a level look. "I can't imagine an artifact thief resorting to violence, but we can't forget that Joey was attacked in the barn. I certainly think the dig site is safe enough."

Roy nodded. "She's smart and talented and inexperienced."

"If you're wanting to know what I know of Brett, the answer is nothing. He's a difficult man who's devoted to his work."

Roy put his hard hat back on, shading his eyes. "I saw Millie was up here. I guess she's checking it out, too."

"Yes, she went up to look at the mound."

"And assess Brett Gibson, I'm sure," Roy said. "Well, there's one thing for certain there. If Millie gets a whiff of anything unsavory about Brett, she'll have Regina on a tour of Europe or going to school in France or whatever it takes to protect her."

For some reason Rebecca took no solace in Roy's assessment of his sister-in-law. Protecting a child was one thing, but Millie sounded as if she might go a little overboard.

"Look, there's the sheriff," Roy said, nodding toward the drive where the patrol car eased toward them. "I have to say, Dru's giving this case a lot of his personal attention." He grinned. "He's a good man, Rebecca. Everyone in the county thinks so. Or almost everyone. A man who enforces the law is always going to have some detractors." He waved at the crane operator and hurried away to give new directions.

Rebecca still held the list in her hand as she walked toward the patrol car. Dru was getting out, and at the sight of his lean body, she felt a tingle rush through her. Flashes of the night before were like pulses of electric shock as she remembered his lips, his hands, the way his body felt pressed against hers.

"Are you okay?" Dru asked, putting out a hand to steady her when she drew abreast of him.

"I'm not sure," she said, smiling. "I think I'm suffering from last-night-traumatic-shock syndrome. I keep remembering…things."

Her words had a powerful effect on Dru. His hand on her arm tightened involuntarily and he stepped closer. "I'm here on official business, ma'am, and I can't have any of that kind of talk. It distracts me."

For a moment, Rebecca could think of nothing more important than rushing back to the cottage for more of the wonderful distraction Dru was talking about. But then she saw something flicker in his eyes.

"What's wrong?" she asked.

"It's John Ittawasa. He's upset that the dig site was abandoned last night. He wants to halt the dig until he can be assured that security measures have been established."

"Damn Brett," Rebecca said vehemently. "He's more trouble than he's worth. I told him this could happen."

"He's a man who acts first and thinks later, that's for sure."

"And he's acted himself right into a corner." Rebecca realized she was still holding the list of names Roy had given her. She handed them to Dru, explaining what they were.

His gaze scanned down the list and stopped, his brow furrowing. "Who is this Frederick Lee?" he asked.

Rebecca shook her head. "That's some new man hired to work on the house." Rebecca felt Dru withdrawing. His posture even changed. "What's going on?" she asked.

"I'll be back," he said. "I need to speak with Roy and Eugene for a moment."

He didn't offer any explanations but walked brusquely away, his jaw grim and his gaze focused on the work crew building the house.

DRU SCANNED the workers, looking for a familiar face. When he finally saw his brother, he felt the expected sense of dread. His brother's name was Frederick Lee Colson. It wasn't uncommon for Freddy to use an alias when it suited his purposes.

Freddy was directing the crane as it placed a huge block in the growing wall of the house. Dru watched him for a moment. His brother was a bit shorter, more muscular, and with light-brown hair. Features that would be considered handsome were marred by a scar on one cheek.

Once the block was settled, Freddy hopped down from the wall and sauntered over. "Hey little brother," he said, grinning. "I wondered how long it would take for you to hear I was in town."

"Why didn't you give me a call?" Dru asked, knowing the answer. Freddy had worried their father into an early grave.

"I didn't figure you were all that interested in talking over old times," Freddy said, wiping his face with a bandana. "It's hot as hell here. I should have thought this through a little better and stayed in Montana for the summer."

"Why are you home?" Dru asked, getting right to the heart of the matter.

"Why not?" Freddy countered. "I've got as much right to be here as you."

Dru stared into his brother's face. They'd fought as kids, and that childhood dislike hadn't softened as adults. Freddy had done everything he could as a teenager to make life difficult for their father Stuart Colson.

"I see you've stepped into the old man's shoes," Freddy said, pointing at the badge on Dru's chest. "You always gave your all to please the old man."

"He wasn't that hard to please," Dru said, feeling the anger begin to surge.

"Maybe not for you, but it sure didn't work like that for me. I couldn't draw a breath without bringing down the wrath of God."

Dru knew there was no point in going over the same old, tired arguments. "When you finish up today, stop by the office."

"No thanks. I don't have a lot of good memories of the sheriff's office."

"It wasn't a request."

"What? You're going to repeat the old man's life and arrest me?"

Dru felt his jaw clenching. "If I have to. But right

now, I just need to ask you some questions. I'd rather do it when you finish up for the day, unless you want to go now."

Freddy glanced around and saw that both Roy and Eugene Batson were watching them. "I don't need to lose this job."

"You might, when they realize you're using a false name."

"It's my legal name now. I got it changed. I don't have the pride in the Colson name that you do."

"I'll be waiting for you," Dru said, walking away before his temper got the better of him.

## CHAPTER TEN

SWEAT TRICKLED down Rebecca's back. She'd watched the scene between Dru and the construction worker and knew there was something between the two men. Anyone watching could have seen it. But when Dru returned, he didn't say anything at all, and she didn't press him. Now they stood at the dig site, waiting for Brett to give them an audience. Dru was growing impatient, and Rebecca felt her nerves snapping, one at a time.

"Winston," she called out to the man who documented the finds, "please tell Brett we need to speak with him. Now." Brett was as touchy as a cat with sore paws and she didn't want to approach his dig site with Dru in tow. They'd had more than one discussion about the need for total privacy at the site, but she'd been waiting long enough.

"I think they may be on to something big," Winston told her in his easy drawl. "They've been hunkered over that hole for the past three hours. They didn't even stop for a coffee break."

"I don't care if they think they've found Ponce de Leon himself, tell Brett to come over here." She was tempted to say more, but she restrained herself.

When Brett finally came over, his face was alight with happiness. "You have to see this," he said, grabbing her hand. His actions were impatient and insistent, and Rebecca saw Dru edge forward, as if to intervene.

"Whatever is so important will have to wait. You've got us in a lot of trouble, Brett. John Ittawasa wants to close down the dig."

"Not after he sees this," Brett almost crowed. "I've found it, Rebecca. This is the discovery that's going to make me famous and Blackthorn a historical shrine."

Rebecca could feel the energy in Brett. She'd never seen him so animated or so happy. "What is it?"

Brett glanced at Dru but he didn't bother to voice an objection to the lawman being there. "Come see," he said. "It's a good thing the sheriff is here. I want an escort to take this to the bank. I've given it a lot of thought, and perhaps we should get some kind of armored car up here to take it."

Rebecca was stunned by Brett's about-face. Only yesterday he'd fought the idea of putting the artifacts in a bank vault. Now he wanted a law enforcement escort? What was going on?

Infected with Brett's enthusiasm, she and Dru hurried to the site that had been marked off, sectioned, labeled and slowly removed, one layer of dirt at a time. When she arrived at the deepest section of the dig, she stopped and stared at the black wooden stick that had been brushed free of dirt, though it remained in the place it had rested. She knelt beside the stick and stared at it. There were decorative designs cut into the black bark, and the thorns that were a part of the tree from which it had been made were still in evidence.

"What is it?" she asked, glancing up at Brett. Dru was kneeling down at the edge of the pit, staring intently at the stick.

"It's the scepter for the king of the Mound Builders. It's the symbol of his authority to rule his people. It was called the Black Stick, and it was made from the biggest of the thorn trees, possibly from the very thicket that grows on this estate. That's probably why the king chose to be buried here. It's the source of his power." Brett was almost dancing with glee. "We've found the grave, Rebecca. We have an incredible find. That scepter was buried with the last king of the Mound Builders. We've done it!"

For one split second, Rebecca let herself float with the joy of the find. Brett had researched and studied the history of the Mound Builders. He and his crew had been steadily excavating the mound with extreme care. This find would greatly please Marcus and Aurelia.

"Congratulations, Brett," she said, accepting the hand that Dru held down to help her out of the pit. "There's only one complication."

"What's that?" Brett asked, undaunted by her naysaying.

"John Ittawasa can close this site. And if he does, it's going to be your fault." She took no pleasure in watching the happiness disappear from Brett's features. The mask of barely suppressed anger dropped back into place.

"Ittawasa can't stop this dig. He'd have to go to the federal level."

"And he will," Rebecca warned. "And Brett, you have no one to blame for this but yourself. In your little fit of temper last night, you left yourself wide open. Now Dru has arranged for us to all get together. I highly recommend that you eat a little crow, apologize for leaving the site unguarded, and beg for forgiveness."

"I will not—"

"Then prepare to be fired," Rebecca said calmly. "I can't afford for the person in charge of the dig to antagonize the local people or the Indians. I don't want to fire you, Brett, but I will."

"You can't do that." The strident voice came from the base of the mound, and Rebecca walked over to look down at Regina Batson. The young woman was climbing with a vengeance. When she reached the top, she ignored everyone except Rebecca. "You can't fire Brett. He's the one who started the dig and he should be allowed to finish it."

"I need a reliable employee," Rebecca said. "Brett pulled a stupid stunt last night, and now he's being forced to answer for it. He can apologize and make it good enough that John Ittawasa believes him, or he can walk."

She kept her gaze on Brett as she spoke and she saw the muscle clench and unclench in his jaw. "I'll apologize," he finally said. "It was foolish to bring all the men into town. I'll tell him that."

A look of relief passed over Dru's face and made

Rebecca want to smile. Instead, she kept her face stern. "You've done some terrific work, Brett, and I want you to have all the credit for it, but I need you to do what we agreed."

"You've got it," Brett said, dropping back into his normal surly tones. "Just keep all of those outsiders away from my dig site. I won't be blamed again for the loss of an artifact."

The words hung in the air for a moment before Dru spoke. "My office at three, sharp."

"I'll be there," Brett assured him.

DRU PACED his office, glancing at the computer every few seconds to see if anything new could be found on Frederick Lee Colson, alias Fred Lee. When the screen blinked to life, he checked through his brother's criminal record, relieved to find that Freddy had been paroled for good behavior and had, so far, maintained a clean record.

He looked up to find Lyle standing in the doorway. "Freddy's working at Blackthorn, on the Batson construction crew," he said.

Lyle's eyebrows shot up. "I guess Eugene and Roy were off at college when Freddy started his crime spree around town. I don't think they'd hire him if they knew."

"He's using a different name. He had it legally changed. Fred Lee."

"He had his name changed?" Lyle's mouth tightened. "That boy. I can't imagine what turned him around like it did." Lyle's eyes widened. "You know, I just remembered something, Dru. Might be something important."

"What?" Dru watched Lyle closely. The older deputy was a professional, a man who'd seen almost everything, and he seldom got excited. But he was humming with energy.

"Freddy and Randall Levert were good friends. They both did sort of an about-face during one summer. I never put it together because Randall became such a mama's boy. Freddy, he became a juvenile delinquent. But the thing is, they both changed over the course of that one summer."

"What summer would that be?" Dru asked, feeling a connection in his gut.

"I can't say off the bat, but let me do a little poking around in the case files and I'll come up with something for you by the end of the afternoon."

"Thanks, Lyle," Dru said, putting his arm around the deputy's shoulders. "Dad always told me to rely on you."

"Your old man was a good sheriff, Dru. He was a lot like you in temperament. It was always a wonder that he got re-elected every time, because he didn't play favorites with all the big money. But the common people loved him. Even when he put their kids in jail. Maybe because he had to do the same thing to his own kid."

"It seemed as though Freddy was determined to make Dad choose between him and his integrity. He'd break the law and not even attempt to explain why he did it. I'll never understand why Freddy hated Dad so."

"You'll probably never get the straight of that. I doubt Freddy knows why. I suspect it has something to do with your mama's death, though the good Lord knows Stuart did everything he could to save her. Back in those days breast cancer was a death sentence. There just wasn't anything to be done. By the time they figured out what was going on, it was way too late. But your dad took her to every expert he could find."

"I remember," Dru said, and he did. Though he seldom visited those memories of his mother's fatal illness. He preferred to remember her in the kitchen, laughing as she dumped too much food coloring in cake icing, or meeting them after school in roller skates so she could skate home with them. "Freddy knows all of this as well as I do."

"He may know it, but he may still want to blame someone. Dru, you always had your dad. The two of you were like two peas in a pod. Maybe Freddy felt like he didn't have anyone after your mom died."

"Freddy walked away from Dad and from me."

Lyle patted his shoulder. "I'll check back in the old records and find Freddy's first offense. He was a juvenile, so nothing was done, but I'll bet I can find some mention of it. That should give us a date to start working with."

"I've got a meeting in the boardroom at three," Dru said. "Before that, I'm running over to Ella's for some lunch. Can I bring you something back?"

"Sure, I'll take the special of the day—whatever it is."

Dru didn't wait for the money Lyle was pulling out of his pocket. He walked out into the heat and the sunshine and tried to walk away from the feelings of anger and loss that seemed to hover just above his shoulders.

ELLA'S PLACE was hopping when he walked in and took a seat at the counter. He ordered a lunch special for himself and one to go for Lyle and sipped the sweetened iced tea that Ella put in front of him.

"I need to talk to you," Ella said as she bustled around the café.

"What's going on?" he asked.

"I was drinking my coffee this morning and I found myself up at Blackthorn."

Dru was familiar with Ella and her visions. Had anyone else approached him with such a tale, he would have laughed out loud. But more than once, Ella had been helpful in solving cases. She made no claims to be able to see the past or the future, but sometimes she did see details that added up to plenty.

"You were at Blackthorn, too," she said, lowering her voice. "It was just a brief flash, but I saw you standing on a bluff with the sun strong in your face. You were looking at someone, but he was only a shadow because of the sun. But whenever you moved, he moved. It was a mirror image of yourself. But this other person was dark, angry."

The confrontation with Freddy came back to Dru. Ella was describing an event that had already happened, but he had no intention of stopping her. He wanted to hear what else she might add.

"I tried to get between the two of you because I knew there was going to be trouble, but I couldn't. It was as if some force bound the two of you together and I couldn't step inside it."

"What did happen?" Dru asked.

"Nothing, really," Ella said, relief in her eyes. "But it was a strong emotion, Dru. I came back to myself at the kitchen table and I was going to call you today if you didn't stop by here."

"Was anyone else in the vision?"

She thought a minute. "I can't recall anyone else. But I wasn't paying much attention to anything except you and that dark stranger."

Dru sipped his tea. "Freddy's back in town. I met him this morning at Blackthorn."

"Oh," Ella said, sorrow touching her face. "I had hoped he might not come back here. This place has held only pain for him."

"Most of it self-created pain."

"While that may be true it doesn't make it any less painful, Dru. I remember Freddy when he was ten years old and riding his bicycle all over town. You would tag along with him and I can't tell you the times he would stop and wait for you to catch up, or grab your shirttail as you tried to ride out into the street without looking. He was good to you for many years."

Dru did remember those times, but somehow they

had nothing to do with the brother he had now. That Freddy had vanished long ago.

"He made his choices and he nearly killed Dad with them."

Ella patted Dru's hand on the counter. "You see Freddy again, you tell him to come by here. That boy loved blueberry cobblers and I just got a flat of berries in from Clancy, Alabama. Tell him Ella's going to bake him up a cobbler."

Dru couldn't help smiling. Ella never gave up on someone once she loved them. It was one of the constants that had made life bearable when he'd lost his mother. "I'll tell him," he said, and he would. Whatever lay in the past between him and Freddy, he'd never deny his brother the bit of comfort that Ella offered.

He finished his lunch and picked up the bag of food that had been prepared for Lyle. It was time to get back to work.

REBECCA SLIPPED a red sleeveless top on and tucked it into beige Capri slacks that showed off her figure very well. She slid her feet into woven leather mules and took a look in the slightly warped mirror hanging in the cottage. She looked casual yet professional, exactly the image she wanted to strike.

This meeting with John Ittawasa was important, but it wasn't a "suit-and-stockings" kind of meeting. In fact, there were few such meetings in Natchez in the summer. One thing she was growing to love about the small city was the reasonable approach to clothes and the seasons. Folks knew how to look sharp yet dress cool.

She applied a light coat of lipstick, admitting to herself that she was nervous about the meeting. If Brett lost his temper and played the fool, which he had a tendency to do, then she'd have to make good on her promise to fire him. Despite his surly nature, she didn't want to do that. Brett worked hard. He'd put a lot of himself into this project. But one way or the other, he was going to have to learn to control his temper.

Niggling at the back of her mind was the way Dru had simply gotten in his car and driven back to town. He'd been distracted, and there had been something dark in his normally clear eyes. She'd felt his withdrawal like a physical thing, rather than emotional, and it troubled her that she was already so vulnerable when it came to him. She'd decided to confront him directly about what was bothering him. She'd learned long ago that the best way to handle a problem was to tackle it head on, not to dodge it.

The Black Stick had been carefully removed from the gravesite and was being dusted and studied. Brett had been reluctant to leave it, but he wanted it thoroughly cleaned, photographed and examined before he turned it over for safekeeping.

To that end, he'd left it with Winston and Regina. Both had vowed not to let it out of their sight for a split second. Still, Rebecca would have preferred to take it straight to the bank vault. She was gun-shy after the loss of the bowl. She gave her image one last quick glance in the mirror and started toward the cottage door to wait for Brett on the porch.

She wasn't surprised when Brett pulled up in front of the cottage and blew the horn instead of getting out and coming to the door like a gentleman. Brett was a long way from understanding the refinements of being a gentleman—or women's attraction to them. Dru, on the other hand, seemed to be a natural gentleman.

Even at the thought of him she felt a ripple of excitement course through her body. If she wanted to play with fire, she could allow herself a few brief memories from the night before. Just one was enough to send the blood rushing to her cheeks, and when she got into the passenger side of the vehicle, Brett gave her a curious look.

"We haven't got all day," he said impatiently.

She ignored him and buckled her seatbelt. She was tempted to give him another stern warning but decided that she'd done her best. Brett would either behave or not. It was up to him to save his job.

"How long will we be gone?" he asked as he headed to town.

"That depends on you," she answered, her gaze out the window as she enjoyed the sight of the old river town washed in the afternoon sunlight. From several vantage points she could catch a glimpse of the river. The mighty Mississippi, gateway to the world for much of the South during one point in history. The river was still a major thoroughfare for river traffic, but it wasn't the vital link that it had once been.

Brett parked and to her surprise came around to hand her out of the car. He was nervous, and she hoped it would work to keep him civil and pleasant.

At the courthouse they went directly to the board-room where Dru was already waiting with John. Both men stood as she entered, and when they sat down at the empty table, Rebecca was prepared to defend the need to continue to dig.

Rebecca spoke first, followed by Brett. The archae-ologist gave a detailed account, with illustrations, of how the dig was going. To Rebecca's surprise, he didn't mention the Black Stick.

"In conclusion, I want to take full responsibility for leaving the burial mound unattended," Brett said. "It was foolish and childish, a very bad decision on my part. It won't happen again, I promise."

John's features didn't soften, but he did place his hands on the table and leaned forward as he began to speak. "The men I sent to guard Blackthorn have no intention of interfering with your work. But this is per-haps the last chance for the history of my people to be truly explored. I can't afford to let thieves make off with it."

"I understand," Brett said with a hint of contrition in his voice. "I made a big mistake. I'm just lucky nothing worse happened."

"I don't trust in luck," John said.

"Then you have my word that the mound will be guarded every night if you don't move to shut us down. In fact, I have a plan that might prevent future burglaries," Brett said, a grin spreading over his face.

Rebecca felt her gut knot. So Brett had some big scheme hatched. She should have known better than to trust him to be a grown-up.

"We discovered something of vital importance today," Brett said, his demeanor changing to one of swagger. "We found the Black Stick that was the sign of the Mound Builder's king. We've positively identified the mound at Blackthorn as the final resting place of King Wenabitta. We are going to make history. To that end I propose a huge press conference where we reveal the stick and discuss the historical significance of the mound at Blackthorn."

Rebecca briefly closed her eyes. Brett was a total fool. She looked at John and saw the anger in his face. This wasn't the proper way to inform him that a significant discovery had been made.

"Brett found the Black Stick only an hour or so ago," she said, leaning forward. "His men are cleaning it up now. I'm sure you want to see it."

"You left it at Blackthorn?" John asked, his voice cold.

"In the care of several trusted employees," Rebecca said soothingly. "Our intention was to take you there and show you personally, but Brett couldn't manage to keep such a fabulous secret." She shot him a look daring him to open his mouth. When she looked at Dru, she saw that he was hiding a smile at her quick diplomacy.

"Are you positive it's the stick that symbolizes the power of leadership?" John asked.

"That's one reason we're so eager for you to see it," Rebecca said. "I think you'd be the best person to make that identification."

"And my plan to have a big press party to announce the find will be the perfect celebration," Brett broke in. "We'll have national media attention, and that will insure that no burglar will try to steal more artifacts."

"How do you figure that?" Dru asked lazily. "You think the TV cameras will stay at Blackthorn permanently? Sort of your own personal Discovery Channel show on unearthing bits of pottery and bone?" Dru's voice was laced with sarcasm.

"Once the find is documented," Brett said angrily, "it would make it almost impossible for a person to sell artifacts stolen from the site."

"Except to a private collector," John said in a monotone. "There are people who would prefer that the Native American past remain unexplored."

Rebecca felt a chill. She'd never considered such a thing. But there were racists everywhere, and surely there were some who would prefer to have the original inhabitants of the area permanently forgotten.

"I don't know about a press conference," she said quickly, "but why don't we go take a look at Brett's find. We can talk about the next step after that." She dug her fingernail into Brett's hand when he started to say something else. It was enough to silence him, but she knew it wouldn't last for long. Brett seemed determined to destroy the excavation of the mound.

A cold dread touched her skin at the thought. She cast a furtive glance at Brett, who was seated again and in his normal mode of pouting.

The stolen bowl had been taken from Brett's tent when it was supposedly under his care. Brett had hired all of the work crew that had access to his tent. Brett had left the mound site unattended deliberately. And now Brett was doing everything in his power to aggravate John Ittawasa. Was it possible that Brett was trying to sabotage the dig?

She glanced at Dru and read almost the exact same questions in his face. He was watching Brett with a cool calculation.

"Shall we go?" John asked, breaking the heavy silence that had fallen over the room.

"Yes," Rebecca said, rising. She needed to move, to walk and think through the horrible suspicion that had occurred to her. And she was eager to get back to Blackthorn and have the Black Stick taken to the safety of a bank vault. "Let's go."

## CHAPTER ELEVEN

"It *is* the Black Stick," John pronounced as he held the artifact in gentle hands. "You've found it, Dr. Gibson."

Rebecca stood slightly back as the two men bent over the thing that each treasured for different reasons. It seemed impossible, but at last they'd found some common ground.

Glancing out of the tent flap, she looked for Dru. He'd come to Blackthorn with them, but then he'd walked up to the construction site.

What was it that drew him up there? Judging from the look on his face, it wasn't something pleasant. It likely involved the man he'd been talking to. Rebecca felt a tingle of worry. Had Dru found someone he suspected of being a thief? Surely he would have told her.

She saw Eugene Batson walk out onto the highest point of the construction and signal to the crane operator to hoist another block.

Even in the short time they'd been in town, the walls of the house had grown radically. The big blocks were now stacked some ten feet high, and workers were scurrying around, preparing to add another layer. If she'd had nothing else to do, she would have gotten a chair and a glass of tea and watched the process. It was fascinating. But her duties required her to referee Brett and John.

"But the press conference is an excellent idea!"

Brett's strident voice called her attention back to the interior of the tent.

"There will be no press conference," John said without inflection. "I have made my decision."

"You aren't the boss of this project," Brett began. "My reputation is on the line here. I deserve to be credited with what I've done."

Rebecca saw the argument was escalating beyond safe levels. The two men were like oil and water. She stepped forward. "I have to agree with John," she said. "We can have a press conference, Brett, and one that is designed to show off the hard work you've done. But not now. Not until we're secure in the fact that someone isn't trying to deliberately ruin the dig." She remembered her concerns in the boardroom that Brett might be just that person.

"I'll take the Black Stick to the bank," John said, reaching for it.

Brett stepped between him and the artifact. "No, I don't think you will. I'm going to have that photographed and documented, and I'm going to have it done with me holding it. I won't be cheated out of my find."

Rebecca sighed. Brett was acting like a paranoid fool, but it was strictly in line with the type of behavior he'd displayed for the duration of her work with him.

"Mr. Ittawasa, we'll get the Black Stick to the vault this afternoon. You have my word on it. Just let Dr. Gibson take his photographs."

"You assume responsibility?" John asked pointedly.

"One hundred percent."

"And nothing will be released to the news media?" John asked.

She understood his concerns. If Brett was taking pictures, there was no guarantee one of those photos might not "leak" out. "I'll handle the film processing, too. Personally."

John nodded. "Please keep me informed."

"I'll do that," she said, walking out of the tent with him.

The meeting had gone more smoothly than she'd dared hope. Another hurdle crossed. She walked John to his car and stood in the drive as he disappeared. She'd narrowly avoided John demanding that the dig be closed, but he was as excited about the Black Stick as Brett. That was about the only thing working in her favor.

Now she had to decide what to do about Brett. Her suspicions made her head pound. It was awful to suspect someone she had to rely on. But Brett's behavior surpassed self-destructive. She had to take into account that he might be deliberately working against the dig.

But why?

That was the question to which she had no answer. At least not yet.

She heard the crunch of gravel and turned to find

Dru almost at her side. She gave him a smile that he returned with full wattage, erasing for a moment the darkness that lingered in his eyes.

"I've got something to check back at the office," he said. "Where are the construction workers staying?"

"One of the local motels. The River Holiday, I think," she said. "Roy or Eugene takes them into town at the end of the day and brings them up in the morning."

"Thanks," he said, once again frowning.

"Are you okay?" Rebecca asked, determined not to push any harder. Dru would tell her when he was ready to do so.

"I'm fine." He brushed a silky strand of her hair from her cheek. "There are some things I need to talk to you about."

"I'm all ears."

He shook his head. "It's a long story and one I don't want to get into now. I need something from you, though."

"What's that?"

"A promise that you'll have dinner with me tonight."

"I'd love to," she said. "There are some things I need to talk to you about, too."

"Yes, I think we have some ground to cover," he agreed.

She wanted to detain him, but there was an edginess she'd never seen in him. Something was troubling him, a lot.

"I'll pick you up about seven," he said. "We'll determine the menu then."

He slipped his arms around her and gave her a big hug. "You're the best thing that's happened in my life in a long time, Rebecca."

"You silver-tongued devil," she teased, glad to see that his mood was brightening up.

"I haven't seen Joey today," Dru said as he started walking to his patrol car. "What's he up to?"

"That's one of the many chores I have left for the afternoon. I'm headed up to his place to check the horses and see what's keeping him so quiet. It isn't like him to miss out on excitement."

"He's probably putting in blueberry bushes or something."

"He does have a green thumb. One that I envy."

"He just knows how to talk to the plants. Are you sure you don't want me to hang around and go with you to take the artifact to the vault?"

"Brett is going to milk this for all it's worth. He's got at least another hour of photography lined up. We'll be fine. In fact, I'm going to take a ride. Then I'll go with him to the vault."

Dru got in his car and waved as he drove away. Rebecca watched him for a moment and then turned to walk to the stables. Joey had been very quiet. Either he was terribly engaged in a project or Brett had been mean to him again. She sighed, hoping it was the former.

DRU GOT ON his radio as soon as he was out of earshot of Rebecca and called Lyle at the office.

"What did you find on my brother?" he asked.

"It was the summer of 1975," Lyle said. "He was caught shoplifting from Ratliff's Drug Store. Nothing serious, just some aftershave."

"That was the year Mom died," Dru said.

"Sure was. While I was at it, I did a little checking on Randall Levert, but I came up with nothing. Like I said, he went from an average kid to a real mama's boy. Up until this business with Yvonne Harris and his mother, he's never been in a lick of trouble."

"Lyle, could you do me a favor?"

"You're the boss."

"Head over to the local newspaper and look through the back issues for that summer. I'm wondering what else went on that might have impacted those two kids."

"Good idea, Dru."

"I'd do it myself, but I think it'll cause less of a stir if you do it."

"I'm reading you loud and clear. Look, though, it's nearly five. I'll probably wait until Monday."

Dru checked his watch and bit back his disappointment. It was four-thirty. The newspaper office closed at five, and it would be silly to go over with only a few minutes to look.

"Good plan. First thing Monday."

"It's on my list."

"I'm headed back in. I'll be there shortly."

REBECCA WALKED through the garden that Joey had worked so hard on, amazed that plants he'd put in the ground only a few days before were already showing signs of growth. Joey was a true gardener. He lavished the plants with love, and they thrived on his attention.

"Joey!" she called his name, trying to remember the last time she'd seen him. "Joey!"

When he stood up, she was almost on top of him. She gasped and stepped backward.

"Sorry, Rebecca," he said. "I was putting in some marigolds around the okra. Keeps the bugs out, you know."

"Where have you been?" she asked.

"Working. And Brett told me if I came near his dig he'd skin me alive."

Anger washed over her, but she didn't let Joey see it. "Brett won't hurt you, Joey. He just likes to talk like an idiot."

"He acts like he'd do it."

"He's a bully, but I want you to tell me the next time he threatens you or says anything mean to you. I've just about had it with him and his attitude."

"I don't want to go up to his old dig anyway. They're digging up dead people." He made a face. "I wouldn't do that. The dead don't want to be disturbed."

Joey said it with such authority that Rebecca felt a chill down her spine. "It may seem strange, but in the long run it'll help us learn a lot about a culture that's long been gone."

Joey shook his head. "I wouldn't do it."

Rebecca linked her arm through Joey's and asked for a tour of his garden. In another few minutes she had him laughing, his concerns for the dead forgotten.

"I'm going into town tonight with Dru. Have you got enough to eat?"

"Plenty. And good stuff, too. Tomorrow I'm going to breakfast at Miss Ella's. Freddy's going to take me."

"Freddy?"

"He works on the construction site," Joey confided. "He's Dru's brother."

Rebecca stopped and faced Joey. "Dru has a brother?" She was totally stunned. Why hadn't Dru told her he had a sibling working at Blackthorn? It didn't take a rocket scientist to put two and two together. He must have been the man Dru was talking to earlier.

"Yeah. Freddy. He said he was the black sheep of the family. He said he was the opposite of Dru."

"How well do you know Freddy?" Rebecca asked.

"He's my new friend. He comes over and talks to me when he's on break. And he's going to take me to breakfast. Saturday is the special day for French toast. Ella makes the best."

"Joey, could you point Freddy out to me?" Rebecca asked as she directed their steps toward the construction site.

"Sure. He's the one high up there on the wall."

Rebecca shaded her eyes with her hand and glanced up. The sun was on the descent and she had a good view of the tall, lean man who stood on top of the wall. He saw her looking and gave a wave.

Joey waved back, grinning. "I like Freddy. He's nice to me."

"That's good," Rebecca said, not sure why Dru hadn't told her his brother was on the construction crew. "If you need anything from town, call and tell me. I'll pick it up for you."

"Sure thing, Rebecca. Are you going to ride?"

"I shouldn't take the time, but I'm going to." It was true. She had plenty to do, but the idea of a short ride sounded like the perfect plan. "In fact, I think I owe it to Mariah."

REBECCA GROOMED the buckskin until her golden hide was burnished. She saddled up and set off through the woods of Blackthorn at an easy trot. Of the three horses, Mariah was the easiest going. Rebecca let her imagination wander as she moved beneath the leafy branches of the trees. Despite the heat, there was no place more beautiful than the Blackthorn woods.

The trail opened to a long straightaway and Mariah picked up a canter without any urging. Rebecca sat back and enjoyed the ride. In a few moments, she found herself playing the imaginary games that were part of a good ride for her.

In her mind it was just after the War Between the States. The landscape didn't change, but she was wearing a dark riding habit and a mask. At her side was a sword in a scabbard. She was Andre Agee's assistant. The local folks called her...Satana. She smiled at her own foolish fancy.

She was on the trail of a rich carpetbagger, a man she intended to unburden of his wealth so that she could redistribute it to the poor people from whom he'd stolen it.

The trail ahead was clear, but she allowed her imagination to create another rider, a man fleeing from her. He looked back over his shoulder and fear was plain upon his face. He knew the reputation of Satana—and he was riding for his life.

Leaning forward into Mariah's black mane, Rebecca urged the mare to greater speed. Eager to go, Mariah surged forward into a full gallop.

Rebecca played the game, pursuing the imaginary man, until she felt Mariah begin to slow. Sitting back up, she brought the mare down to a trot and then a walk. It had been a glorious adventure while it lasted. Too bad her target had gotten away. But next time, she'd get him.

She took a deep breath, determined not to think about Dru and his brother. She had to wait until tonight to give him a chance to tell her in his own time. It was growing late and she needed to get back to Blackthorn to take the Black Stick to the vault.

The shortest trail home led off to the right and Rebecca took it. She'd had a wonderful half hour and she felt refreshed and invigorated, but there was much to do before her date.

Her impulse was to put Mariah into a canter and get home as fast as possible, but the mare was blowing and needed to cool down. Rebecca maintained a walk. She had plenty of time to finish everything that needed to be done.

When the wailing cry of the baby started up, Rebecca felt an unpleasant surge of adrenaline. Mariah heard it, too, and the mare stopped, her ears pointed forward as she turned to the woods on the right side of the road.

The cry seemed near. So near she had to investigate. She slipped from the saddle to the ground and dropped the reins.

The keening cry of the baby sliced into her. Even though she knew it couldn't be a real infant, she found chill bumps dancing on her skin. The baby's cry seemed filled with all the woe and pain of the world.

Careful to avoid stepping on sticks, she made her way silently into the woods.

The sound seemed to be coming from a dense thicket of scrub brush on the lip of a small ravine. Rebecca made her way there, moving as silently as she could. Whoever was doing this was going to pay. That was all she could think about as she inched forward.

The woods had grown terribly quiet except for the recorded cry of the infant. It was a creepy quiet, as if all living creatures held their breath to see what would come next. For once, Rebecca could have done without her over-active imagination. This was no time to be conjuring up spooky thoughts.

The crying was much louder. She knew she was close to the source. She stepped into the thicket, aware that the close growth of the trees and brush had cut the afternoon light. It was almost as if she'd stepped into twilight.

Pressing forward, she saw something on the ground. At first she didn't recognize the tiny bootee for what it was, but when she did, her heart hammered in her chest.

The delicate knit bootee was banded with a thin pink ribbon. It was the perfect size for a newborn. Someone was going to a whole lot of trouble to set the scene, she thought as she bent to pick up the bootee.

Out of the corner of her eye she saw movement. A figure clad in black darted out from behind a tree. She didn't see what the figure held in its hand until the heavy stick swung through the air toward her.

She tried to dodge backwards, but her boot heel caught on a fallen tree. Still clutching the bootee, she threw up her hands to ward off the blow.

The first strike caught her on the forearm, a blow solid enough to make a loud cracking sound. She gasped in pain. She was still trying to regain her balance and scramble away when she was struck in the back of the head. The severe blow sent her reeling over the lip of the ravine. Crashing through small bushes, limbs and leaves, she tumbled head over heels for what seemed like an eternity. When at last she landed, her face was pressed into the loamy-smelling soil.

For a long moment she fought against the blackness that swirled over her. She knew she had to remain awake, to fight or flee or do something to save herself.

But it was no use. The darkness grew thicker and denser, and finally she slipped beneath it.

# CHAPTER TWELVE

DRU HEARD THE phone ringing while he was in the shower. Without even hesitating, he stepped from beneath the rush of water, grabbed a towel and picked up the receiver. He'd grown up in a law-enforcement family. A ringing phone too often meant someone needed his help. It wasn't something to be ignored.

"We can't find Rebecca!"

Joey's panicked voice seemed to pierce him like a hot wire. "Slow down, Joey. What's happened to Rebecca?" He fumbled over the last question as a million dark possibilities crowded in on him.

"She went riding. Mariah came back, alone. She's hurt!" Joey was almost in tears. "The vet is here stitching her up. He said she was hit with something. Her shoulder's bleeding."

"How long has Rebecca been missing?" Dru had to think professionally. This was his job. He had to distance himself emotionally and work.

"She went for a ride. She said she'd be back in less than an hour." Joey pulled in a long breath. "Mariah came back without her. She ran to the barn and I went to check her. There was blood all down her leg. And I couldn't find Rebecca anywhere. Brett told me not to call you yet but I couldn't wait any longer."

Dru checked his watch. It was six-thirty. No one had had very long to hunt for Rebecca. Maybe she was simply walking back to Blackthorn, only her pride injured by having fallen off her horse.

"Who's hunting for Rebecca?" he asked, pulling on his slacks as he held the phone between shoulder and ear.

"Everyone! Even Brett. He took the truck and drove down all the trails. Rebecca's gone. She's disappeared!" Joey's voice had risen to a near wail.

"She's okay," Dru reassured him. "Joey, stay calm. You have to be able to remember everything. I'm on the way."

And he was. He stepped into his boots and grabbed a shirt, which he buttoned while he ran to the patrol car. As soon as he was on the way to Blackthorn, he radioed for back up and alerted the paramedics to remain on the ready. The picture Joey had painted wasn't a good one.

Using his lights and siren, he sped out of town. He also placed a call to John Ittawasa, tracking him down to the Eola Hotel where he'd checked in the day before. John's quick accessibility was in Rebecca's favor. John was an expert tracker.

"John, this is Dru," he said as soon as John answered the phone. "There's trouble at Blackthorn. I may need your help."

John didn't bother asking questions. He must have

heard the urgency in Dru's voice. "I'll meet you there as quickly as I can."

On the steep trail to the estate, Dru spun gravel on several curves. When he finally pulled in at the campsite of the archaeology team, the faces of the workers told the one story he didn't want to see. Glancing at the construction site, he wasn't surprised to see that all of the workers were gone, except for Regina, who stood almost at Brett's side, her lips white with worry.

He picked up the radio again and got Deputy Press Adkins. "Press, get your tracking dog up to Blackthorn. We've got a missing person who may be seriously injured and we won't have daylight for much longer."

"Wolfer and I are ready to roll," Press assured him.

Dru was hardly out of the car before Joey launched himself in his direction. "You've got to find her, Dru. She's hurt."

"Take it easy, Joey." Dru patted his shoulder. "I'm sure Rebecca simply took a fall. We'll find her in no time and get her fixed up." He had no way of knowing if he was lying to Joey or not, but it was the only thing to say. Joey was distraught.

"We've searched the trails," Brett said. "No sign of her."

"Any sign of a fall or some kind of accident?" Dru asked.

"None."

"There are plenty of places Rebecca could go on horseback that you couldn't get to in a vehicle," Dru said. "Let's hope she was off the trail exploring, dismounted, and something spooked Mariah and sent her running home."

"If Rebecca could walk, she'd be here by now," Brett said angrily. "The men are ready for a search. I figure we can fan out and cover quite a bit of ground." He rubbed at a trace of dirt on his cheek. "I told Rebecca those damn horses were dangerous. She never listened to me. Not even when I was right."

Dru filed the comment away. If Brett was trying to pretend concern, he was doing a good job. The man actually looked worried.

"Joey," Dru said, knowing that the young man needed a job, something that made him feel he was helping. "Would you saddle one of the horses for me? A Western saddle if you have one." He remembered the small English saddle Rebecca had been riding in and sincerely hoped there was a version with a horn in the barn. He heard a truck door slam and felt a sense of relief as John Ittawasa walked toward them.

"What's he doing here?" Brett demanded.

"I called him." That was the only explanation Dru intended to give.

"I'll saddle Cogar. Mariah's hurt." Joey's face clouded. "Or you could ride Diable."

"Cogar will be fine," Dru said. Not that he had anything against the black horse, but anything named devil might be more than he could handle.

"What are you going to do, ride to the rescue like the Lone Ranger?" Brett asked sarcastically.

Dru's answer was cut short by John. "I guess I'll be

Tonto. Saddle the black horse, too," he told Joey. "I'll ride him." John smiled. "I've been wanting an excuse to ride him."

"I'll be back with both of them," Joey said, his anxiety relieved for the moment with a simple but necessary chore to perform.

"John's the best tracker in the Southeast," Dru told Brett and the men who'd gathered around him. "Now I need someone to get an article of clothing from Rebecca's house. My deputy Press is on the way up here with a tracking dog. Give him the clothing, and then y'all organize a search on foot with him."

"All of the construction workers are gone," Regina chimed in, "but I can call my dad and he'll bring them back up here to help."

Dru shook his head. "Thanks, but it might be best if we just keep it confined to those of us here now." He didn't say that he'd need more volunteers in the morning if they didn't find Rebecca soon. He didn't even want to think it. But he did. The last time he'd searched the woods at Blackthorn the end result had been nothing less than tragic.

JOHN DISMOUNTED and knelt beside a series of muddled horse tracks in the middle of the trail. He studied them a moment before he motioned for Dru to dismount.

"Rebecca got off her horse here," he said, pointing to a small indention in the dirt that Dru recognized as a boot heel print.

"You say she got off?" Dru asked.

"Yes, she walked here." He pointed to the distinct marks that ended at the edge of the path where grass was thick. "She was walking into the woods there."

Dru followed the direction in which John pointed. Dusk had fallen and the light was fading fast.

"The horse waited here. Nervous. See how the mare danced over her tracks?"

Dru could read the story as John told it. "I wonder why Rebecca got off."

"I'd say she saw something or heard something," John said. "Or she could have had a call of nature."

"Let's check it out," Dru said, dropping the reins to the ground. He pulled the small but powerful flashlight he'd taken from his car off the saddle horn.

John led the way into the woods, pointing out the almost invisible signs that showed someone had gone that way before. Dru could only thank his lucky stars that John had been staying in Natchez. He had deputies proficient in tracking, but none as good as John.

In the distance, Dru heard the baying of a hound and he knew Press and his dog, Wolfer, had hit a trail. He looked at John.

"I'm worried," John admitted. "Ms. Barrett is an excellent horsewoman. She didn't fall off. She got off. And she went into the woods."

"We could wait for the others to get here. They aren't far behind," Dru said, judging the distance by the clear bay of the hound.

"Or we could go into the woods and look now," John said. "I vote for that."

Together they pushed into the undergrowth. They hadn't gone thirty yards when John put out his hand and stopped Dru. Both men froze as they listened.

Soft moaning came from up ahead. It was an eerie sound that suggested someone in pain. Dru slipped his gun from the holster and together they moved slowly forward.

They were on the lip of the ravine before Dru realized that the ground sloped abruptly away. He turned on the flashlight. He saw her instantly in the beam of light, lying in the bottom of the ravine.

"Rebecca!" He slid down the side, heedless of the branches that slapped at his face and the roots that tried to trap his feet. "Rebecca!" He knelt beside her, feeling for a pulse, his hands moving over her body to check for broken bones as John Ittawasa scrambled down beside him.

"It doesn't feel like anything's broken, but I can't tell about her back," Dru said.

"We need to turn her over. She's suffocating in the leaves."

Very gently the two men eased her over. In the glare of the light, the fresh blood was vibrant and red, and it was surrounded by older blood that had turned a shade of burnt brown.

"Damn," John said, pulling out his handkerchief and pressing it to the wound on her forehead. "We need an ambulance."

Dru didn't wait. He touched the radio on his shoulder.

"This is the sheriff. We need paramedics and an

ambulance at Blackthorn." He could hear the men and dogs headed their way clearly now. "Someone will be waiting to lead you to the victim."

REBECCA'S EYES fluttered open as the stretcher bumped into the ambulance. She saw Dru's worried face, Joey's right behind him.

"Hey," she said, wondering why she was strapped down on a stretcher.

"Rebecca," Dru said, echoed by Joey. "What happened?"

She frowned and felt a million needles in her head. "Where am I?"

The ambulance attendant motioned for Dru to get in or out. "I'm okay," she said, even though she felt as if every bone in her body was cracked.

"I'll follow you," Dru told the ambulance attendant, climbing out and easing Joey with him. "Rebecca, I'll meet you at the hospital."

The doors slammed and Rebecca heard the siren as she was taken away. She found the wail of the siren lulling rather than frightening. She closed her eyes and slept.

DRU SPENT a few minutes reassuring Joey and thanking his deputies, Brett and the crew for their help with the search. He wanted to get to the hospital, but he had a few things to do first. The best way he could help Rebecca was to find out who'd hurt her.

The paramedics had told him that she'd been struck

several times with something heavy. Her left forearm had taken a severe blow, as had her head. She was lucky to be alive.

The only clue that Dru had as to what had happened to Rebecca was the baby bootee she'd had clutched in her hand. He'd been able to remove it only after the medics had given her something to relax her.

Brett and his crew were waiting expectantly. John and Joey left to untack the horses and to check on Mariah. Dru was going to owe John more than thanks. He had a way of soothing Joey that was enviable.

"What happened to Rebecca?" Brett asked. His tone was impatient.

"That's what I intend to find out," Dru said. "All of you were here, at the campsite, correct?"

Brett pointed at the men. "They were at the mound. Regina and I were here, working on some documentation with Winston."

"The construction crew had gone, correct?" he asked.

"They were all gone. They leave at five, on the dot. They get overtime. My crew doesn't," Brett said.

"And you heard nothing? Saw nothing?"

"There was nothing to see or hear," Brett said, growing defensive. "If we'd heard or seen anything we would have gone to help Rebecca." He stepped closer to Dru, his eyes narrowing. "Seems to me you're the one not doing his job. I thought you were going to make sure the trespasser was picked up. Or is that too complicated for a hick town sheriff?"

Dru's fists clenched, but he'd learned long ago that showing his temper never furthered an investigation. Brett wasn't worth the loss of dignity that would result from a fistfight. Not to mention the trouble he could get into if he threw the punch first. "I'll check with the men John posted on the perimeter of the estate and see if they know anything."

"While you're at it, why don't you check and see if maybe one of them hurt Rebecca. I think old John's trying to sabotage this whole operation, and what better way than to take out the project director?"

Dru stared into Brett's eyes. "John Ittawasa isn't that kind of man, but I find it interesting that you'd develop such a scenario. It just lets me know what you're capable of, Gibson. If I suspect anyone here, it's you."

"You'd better back up that kind of talk with evidence," Brett said. "Unless you want a slander suit." He looked at Regina. "You heard him, didn't you?"

Dru didn't even bother looking at the young woman. He kept his gaze on Brett. "I do suspect you, Gibson. Of many things, the least among them of being a complete fool. If you find that slanderous, you get a lawyer and you go to town with your lawsuit."

"Stop it!" Regina stepped between them. "Quit acting like ten-year-olds!"

Dru felt a wash of shame color his face. Regina was right. They were acting like spoiled kids. But there was something about Brett that just brought out the worst in him.

"Thanks, Regina," Dru said as he abruptly walked

away. He'd check with John and the guards he'd posted to see if they knew anything, and then he was going to the hospital.

He found John still talking to Joey, and knew he'd worked wonders when he saw that Joey was actually smiling.

"John said he'd take me to see Rebecca after we call the hospital and they say she can have visitors. He said it was like the time I fell in the barn and got hurt. He said she'd probably be back tomorrow."

"Thanks, John," Dru said, "and I know Rebecca will thank you, too."

When Dru mentioned he wanted to talk to the perimeter guards John had posted, John shook his head. "I've already spoken with them. I stopped by on my way in. They didn't see or hear anything. Whoever came into Blackthorn didn't use the drive or the farm road that comes in from the north."

"Is there any other entrance? I had a man stationed on the river, so no one came in by water."

"I'm sure a determined person could find a million ways in," John said. "But they'd have to go on foot or four-wheeler. There are trails, but they're narrow, overgrown and filled with mud holes that would sink a truck or jeep."

Dru nodded. Blackthorn was a huge estate. It would be impossible to guard the entire perimeter. And John was right. A determined trespasser would find a way in.

"I guess tomorrow I'll get some volunteers and see if we can figure out how the trespasser got in," Dru said.

"I can bring some men."

"I was hoping you'd say that," Dru said with a grin. "I thank you for today, John. You're a talented man."

"I was happy to help. But I am concerned about what's happening here at Blackthorn," John said. "I thought when Yvonne Harris was put in jail this foolishness would end. And when Aurelia and Marcus found the buried treasure, I was hoping the fortune seekers would stay away from here. But now I have to wonder if someone is trying to damage the history of my people."

Dru nodded as he thought. John had good reason to be concerned. "I know Rebecca will do everything she can to protect the mound and all the artifacts."

"Rebecca, yes. But there are others here."

"I know." Dru was ready to leave. He'd found out what he needed to know. Now he needed to talk with the relief deputy at the boat landing, and then he was going to the hospital to see about Rebecca. The paramedic had assured him she wasn't in danger of dying, though her injuries were painful.

"We'll talk later, John. If you have more men, maybe you could double the guards tonight."

"That's already taken care of," John said.

Dru was about to leave the barn when Regina burst through the door. She almost stumbled against him, then glanced around him to see John still there.

"Ah, I need to talk to you," she said, tugging at Dru's sleeve to pull him outside.

Dru was instantly alert. Regina didn't care for him, he knew. She saw him as Brett's adversary, and Regina's loyalty was totally with Brett.

"What can I do for you?" he asked as he followed her outside and into the night.

"It's bad," she said in an urgent whisper. "Really bad."

"What?" Dru tensed. Everything that was happening at Blackthorn seemed tinged with bad.

"It's the artifact."

"The Black Stick?" Dru asked, feeling a full measure of dread. "Rebecca took it to the bank vault."

"No. No, she didn't," Regina said. "Brett was photographing it, and Rebecca went for a ride. She didn't take it. But someone did. It's gone!"

## CHAPTER THIRTEEN

REBECCA FELT THE sharp pain of her bruised rib when she tried to sit up. It almost convinced her that the nurse was right—she wasn't going to be able to get out of bed for a while. But she had to keep trying. She'd asked for a telephone and the nurse had refused. Well, she was going to find one if she had to walk out of the emergency room and locate a pay phone. She had to call Dru or Brett or someone and make them understand that she wasn't able to put the Black Stick in the bank vault as she'd promised John Ittawasa because of the accident.

Though woozy with some of the painkillers they'd given her, she was still plenty capable of understanding the danger of leaving that valuable artifact unprotected at Blackthorn. In fact, she was downright horrified. In the back of her mind, she couldn't help wondering if the entire attack on her wasn't designed to be a distraction so that someone could attempt to take the Black Stick. That awful thought forced her up again. She grabbed the railing and began to pull herself into a sitting position despite the pain.

"Ms. Barrett!" The nurse was standing in the doorway. "You cannot get up."

"Watch me," Rebecca said through gritted teeth. "I have to make a phone call. It's urgent. If you won't bring me a phone, then I'll get up and find one."

The nurse went to her and hesitated. "I'll bring a phone for you if you promise you'll stay in the bed. The doctor would skin me alive if I let you get up. He's going to be angry that you're on the phone. You're supposed to be resting."

"I can't rest as long as I'm worried. One call."

"Okay. I'll be right back. But only if you promise that you'll stay in that bed."

"You have my word."

The nurse returned after only a few moments with a phone and plugged it into a jack by the bed. "I have a feeling I'm going to regret this," she said, handing Rebecca the phone.

"Thanks. I owe you."

"Good. Then I'm taking payment. After this call, you're going to stay quiet and rest."

"Yes, ma'am," Rebecca said, though the woman was her age or younger.

She dialed Dru's cell phone number. At the fifth ring, she was about to give up when she heard him answer.

"Dru, the artifact is still at Blackthorn. Give it to John if he's still there. He can keep it safe."

There was a long pause. "I'm almost at the hospital," Dru said. "We can talk when I get there."

"Don't come here. It's more important—" But Dru had disconnected. Rebecca handed the phone to the nurse and settled back against the pillows. She had the worst feeling that she was too late. Something had already happened to the Black Stick.

RELIEF AT HEARING Rebecca's voice so strong and vibrant was laced with the regret of having to tell her what had happened at Blackthorn. Though he hadn't known Rebecca long, Dru knew her well enough to know that she'd blame herself for the theft.

He pulled into a parking lot and a few moments later he was in the emergency room, checking with the nurses to find out where Rebecca was located. He found her in one of the examining rooms. Her eyes were closed as if she were resting, and he felt a moment of thanksgiving that he'd been given a brief respite from telling her about the Black Stick.

As he stepped through the door, he scanned her body with an intense gaze. Her color was good. There were no casts that he could see. No respirator. He sighed.

"Dru!" Her eyes opened and her clear blue gaze found him and held him. She motioned him over to the bed. "What happened?"

"You tell me," he said, wanting to make sure she was well enough before he told her anything. "We found you in a ravine. The paramedics said it looked as if you'd been struck with something heavy."

"I was." Rebecca frowned. "It's a little hazy, but it's getting clearer. Someone was in the woods, waiting for me. It was almost as if they knew I'd ride by that way."

Dru saw that her body had begun to tremble, and

for one split second he wanted his hands around the throat of the person who'd hurt her and scared her. But he concealed his anger as he went to the bedside and stroked her hand. "Thank God you're okay, Rebecca. Everyone was worried to death about you."

"If I could manage to sit up, I think I could leave," she said, giving him a questioning look.

"Absolutely not!" Dru said. "I will not help you escape the hospital until the doctor releases you."

"Coward," she said, settling back onto the pillows.

Though she talked boldly, Dru could see that she was tired and in pain. He had some questions that he had to ask, though. Reaching into his pocket, he brought out the baby bootee. "Does this bring anything back?"

Rebecca's face lit with memory. "That's it! Now I remember. It was the baby!"

Dru swallowed. If Randall Levert was playing his stupid games again, Dru vowed that the man would find himself in a prison cell. "You heard the crying baby again?" He prompted Rebecca. "What happened after that?"

"It sounded so close. Of course I knew it wasn't a real baby, but I thought if I could find the recording device I could at least confiscate it. And I thought maybe we could figure out who was doing it and make them stop."

"I suspect I know who's doing it, but proving it would be nice." Dru gently rubbed her cool hand. "So you heard the baby. You got off Mariah and left her in the road."

She gave him a curious look. "Yes. I walked into the woods. That's when I saw the bootee on the ground. I bent down to pick it up and someone stepped out from behind a tree."

"Did you get a clear look at who it was?"

Rebecca shook her head. "He...or she...was wearing black. It was a slender person. The face was concealed with one of those black ski masks. I threw up my arm to protect my face but he hit me so hard I fell down. And then he hit me in the side of the head. That's when I fell down the ravine."

Dru felt the anger surge inside him. Rebecca had been ambushed, and from the sound of it, someone had intended to seriously injure her. Dru had a problem, though. The crying baby sounded like Randall Levert; the attack did not. Had Randall, in his deluded state, teamed up with someone else to find the already discovered treasure of Blackthorn? If he had, Randall had no idea how much trouble he was in.

"Rebecca, can you remember anything specific about the person who struck you?"

He continued to rub her hand as she thought. He wanted to smooth away the dark circles under her eyes caused by the pain. Her skin was pale, almost translucent. And whenever she moved, he could tell that she was in pain. Whoever had done this to her was going to pay.

"The person was slender." She shook her head. "A little taller than me." She met his gaze and her eyes were troubled. "I can't remember anything specific."

"It's okay," he said, smoothing her forehead.

"You have to do something for me, Dru. I didn't take the artifact to the bank vault. Will you do it?"

Dru hesitated, but he wasn't going to lie to her. "Rebecca, there's a problem."

If it was possible, she grew even paler. "It's gone, isn't it? I knew it. The whole thing with me in the woods was a distraction."

"Yes, the Black Stick is gone. Someone took it."

"Find them, Dru. We have to get that relic back. We have to."

DRU HAD BEEN GONE twenty minutes when Rebecca finally saw her opportunity. Grasping the bed rail, she pulled herself upright so fast she didn't have time to react to the pain. Once she was sitting, it wasn't that difficult to get to her feet.

Dressing was another matter, but she managed to pull on the riding pants she'd been wearing. Her shirt was bloodstained, but she had no option. It was that or the hospital gown.

Slipping into the boots was easy. She'd have to worry about getting them off later. Standing as upright as her ribs and bruises would allow, she walked carefully past the busy nurses and into the night. It was only then that she realized she didn't have a car or a way to get to Blackthorn. She didn't even have a purse for change to call a cab. If she called Dru, he'd make her go back to the hospital until the doctor released her.

She could call Brett. If she could find a telephone.

She thought of Ella's Café and checked the time. It was after ten o'clock. Ella's was closed.

Dejected, she walked slowly down the long hospital drive, wondering if she dared try her hand at hitchhiking. Behind her a car slowed until it drew even with her. She started walking faster, and the car kept pace.

Glancing over at the Volvo, she was surprised when the passenger window glided down.

"Ms. Barrett?"

She vaguely recognized the voice. "Yes?" She leaned into the window.

"It's me, Millie Batson. Regina's mother. Are you okay?"

"Ah, yes," she said.

"Where are you going?"

Rebecca knew there was no point in lying. It was obvious she was without a ride. "I just left the hospital and I need to get back to Blackthorn. Could you possibly give me a lift to a telephone booth?"

"I can do better than that. How about a ride to Blackthorn?" Millie asked. "Hop in."

Rebecca slid into the passenger seat, amazed at how weak she was. Every time she drew a breath her ribs rebelled. And walking made every one of her limbs feel like dead weight. Perhaps leaving the hospital hadn't been such a bright idea.

"Regina came home this evening terribly upset. She said someone attacked you." Millie turned the car out of the parking lot and accelerated. "Are you okay?"

"Just bruised," Rebecca said.

"You look a little more than bruised, if you don't mind my saying so."

"A couple of cracked ribs. Nothing serious. They'll heal just fine."

"But hurt like the dickens until they do. I was foolish enough to try ice-skating once with Eugene. I hit the ice so hard I cracked two ribs. It was excruciating."

"I'll be fine," Rebecca said with conviction. "Just a few days and I won't even know what happened."

"What did happen?"

Rebecca was a little uncomfortable sharing the story with someone she didn't know, but Millie was Regina's mother. Maybe it would be best to give her the real story instead of a version that had been bandied around the campsite. So she did.

"Who would do such a thing?"

"Good question," Rebecca said.

"You didn't see who it was?"

Rebecca shook her head. "I didn't get a good look. But I have no doubt Dru will figure it out."

Millie laughed. "Everyone in town is talking about what a handsome couple you two make. Dru is quite a catch."

Rebecca didn't answer. She couldn't think of a thing to say that wouldn't sound unfriendly or rude. But she didn't think of Dru as some trophy she'd bagged, and she certainly hoped he didn't feel that way about her.

"Regina seems to have a real involvement in archaeology," she said instead, changing the subject.

"Yes, to her father's growing alarm. He wants her to

follow in his footsteps. To design buildings and leave her mark on the future, not grub around in the past." Millie chuckled. "The two of them are cut from the same hard-headed cloth. It's amazing, and a little scary, to watch them go head-to-head."

"I don't know your husband well, but Regina is very bright."

"Yes, she is. Except maybe where men are involved. She's been so protected. I think maybe Eugene and I made a mistake by not letting her date more when she was younger. She seems fascinated by that archaeologist. What's his name? Brett something."

"Brett Gibson. Yes, I think Regina has a big crush on Brett."

"And does this Brett reciprocate?" Millie asked pointedly.

"That's something you'll have to ask Brett."

"What's he like?" Millie asked. "Regina says he's totally devoted to his work. I've known a lot of men in my day, and none of them were totally devoted to work, if you get my drift."

Rebecca surely did. "I don't know Brett's past. All I can say is that since he's been at Blackthorn, the dig is all that he's been interested in. Several women in town have invited him to dinner or to attend a function, but he's never accepted."

"Then he isn't a rounder."

"I didn't say that," Rebecca said. "I merely told you what I've observed since I've known him."

Millie sighed. "I've invited him to dinner three times and he's declined each invitation. He's always busy. And

I swear, I almost have to go over and pick Regina up long enough to make her come home and take a bath. I'd be lying if I said I wasn't worried."

In listening to Millie chatter on about her daughter, Rebecca had momentarily forgotten her pain. For that she was grateful. "Brett has come to rely on Regina. She's at his side all the time."

"Day and night?" Millie asked, taking a curve too fast.

"That I couldn't say."

"She's too young to realize that her actions can haunt her the rest of her life."

"Youth has no caution," Rebecca agreed. She could see Millie's point and if she were Regina's mother, she'd be concerned, too.

"Should I make Regina come home with me?"

In light of the other things that were happening at Blackthorn—the attacks and robberies—Rebecca didn't know what to say. "Things are going to be a little hectic there for the next few days. It might not be a bad idea for Regina to take a few days off."

"I think so, too. I'm going to insist on it."

"How old is Regina?" Rebecca asked gently.

"She's twenty-one, but she isn't as mature as most girls her age."

"Still, I doubt you can order her home."

"Perhaps not, but I can give it a damn good try."

DRU CRUISED the parking lot of the car dealership, finally having to admit that there was no sign of Randall

Levert. Or anyone else for that matter. It looked as if the business had been abandoned for several days, probably because Randall was holed up in the woods at Blackthorn living out some psychotic fantasy.

At one time, Randall had been a determined salesman. His decline had been so rapid, no one could have predicted it. There had always been a streak of instability in the family, what with Lottie running all over town claiming to be the illegitimate heiress of one of the Agees. But Randall had seemed levelheaded. Solid. Maybe a little withdrawn and shy, but certainly not unstable.

But according to Lyle, Randall had changed from a normal kid to a mama's boy. And another young boy had gone from an honor student to a juvenile delinquent. Another personality change was certainly possible.

Dru was grim as he circled the lot one more time and then drove to the house Randall had shared with his mother, Lottie, before she had been murdered by Yvonne Harris in the woods of Blackthorn a few months before.

The Levert residence showed no sign of life, but Dru got out and repeatedly knocked on the door before giving up. He'd have to have a search warrant to get inside. What would he find in there? More tape recordings of a crying baby? A tiny bootee that matched the one that Rebecca had found in the woods? What did Randall hope to accomplish? Other than, perhaps, to give someone else time to steal a very valuable artifact.

Randall had been used once. He might have found

someone greedy enough to be willing to use him again.

Aggravated that he couldn't find the car salesman, Dru left and headed to the hotel where all of the construction workers were staying. It was going to be a contentious night.

## CHAPTER FOURTEEN

MILLIE PULLED THE Volvo up at the front porch of the cottage. "Do you need some help?" she asked.

"No thanks." Rebecca was actually feeling much stronger. The pain had lessened, and she'd learned that as long as she was standing, she was okay. It was getting up and down that hurt the most.

Rebecca got out of the car. "Thanks, Millie. You were a lifesaver." In the short ride, she'd deduced a number of things about the woman, chief among them Millie's love for Regina and her desire to be a mother that her daughter could be proud of. Natchez was not a town that easily forgave a woman for rising above her roots, but Millie was determined that Regina would never pay the price.

"Keep an eye on my baby," Millie requested. "She's the most important thing in my life."

"I'll do my best." Which wouldn't be much good. At twenty-one, Regina was no baby. But Rebecca didn't have to point that out. Rebecca turned to go inside when Millie stopped her with a question.

"Ms. Barrett, is Regina in physical danger at Blackthorn?"

The one thing Rebecca didn't want was gossip about the thefts getting all over town. She wasn't sure how much detail Regina had told her mother, but Millie was an astute woman. She could sense there was something wrong.

"There are problems at all construction sites. Throw in an archaeological dig and things are bound to happen." She couldn't outright lie, but she could skim over the surface of the truth.

"I ask you again. Is it dangerous?" She took a deep breath. "Maybe it would be a good idea to shut everything down for a while. You know, just pull back. Give things time to settle. I've heard some talk, and folks get worked up over Blackthorn. There are some who still believe the place is haunted. Maybe if you just shut down for a little while, this would all blow over."

Now, that was the one option Rebecca had never considered. To shut down construction would be incredibly expensive. Leaving the dig site unattended would open the door to more vandalism and theft. Millie didn't understand such things. To her, it would seem logical to simply retreat in the face of adversity.

"I'll give it some thought," Rebecca said kindly. "I don't think that's going to be necessary. Everything will work out just fine."

"My husband would understand if you had to stop."

Rebecca wouldn't want to take any bets on that. Blackthorn was a huge project. To pull it out from under Batson and Batson would leave the company with at least a five-month hiatus. Millie's suggestion was offered from the heart, not the pocketbook.

"I'm sure everything is going to be fine here," Rebecca said. "Please don't worry, Millie. If things look the least bit dangerous for Regina, I promise I'll send her home."

"What happened to you in the woods of Blackthorn?" Millie asked. "I'm not interested in gossip, Rebecca. It's my daughter I'm concerned about."

Rebecca wasn't prepared for the question. Millie had caught her off guard. Millie wasn't simply the overprotective mom she'd taken her for. The woman put two and two together and came up with a problematic situation that might pose danger for her daughter.

"I was attacked." Rebecca told the truth but didn't go into any details. "Regina isn't the focus of what's going on at Blackthorn."

"And you are?"

"It would seem so."

"Why?"

Rebecca leaned on the window frame. "I'm not certain, but there are valuable relics in the burial mound."

"So the problems at Blackthorn are motivated by greed?"

"I suspect so," Rebecca said.

"And my daughter camps with the site workers."

"Yes, but no valuable artifacts will remain in the camp. They'll be taken to a safe place, I assure you of that. That removes the motive for anyone to trouble the workers."

Millie smiled at last. "Forgive my pushiness. A mother just has to be sure."

"Good night," Rebecca said, aware of how tired she felt and how leaden her legs were.

"Thanks, Rebecca. It was a pleasure to get to talk with you a little."

Rebecca was inside, the door locked behind her, before Millie could clear the driveway. It was after ten, and Rebecca knew there would be hell to pay in the morning about her unauthorized departure from the hospital.

She ignored the disappointment she felt that Dru wasn't at Blackthorn. He certainly wouldn't know to look for her on the estate since he thought she was spending the night under medical care. But she realized how much she wanted to see him.

And how little she wanted to talk to John Ittawasa. The Indian leader would be furious. And rightly so. The loss of the Black Stick was irreparable. And it was her fault.

She half expected to hear Brett knocking on her door, but she hoped Millie had not gone up to the camp to tell everyone that she was in the cottage. She needed a good night's sleep, but she also felt better at Blackthorn. The place was her responsibility.

And she had to call John.

Sighing, she went to the telephone to place the call

to the Eola Hotel. Putting off the inevitable always cost more in the long run.

When she didn't get a dial tone, she jiggled the switch-hook several times. The line was dead. She smiled in relief. Now everything could wait until the morning, when she was at least a little rested and could think more clearly.

Shutting off the lights, she made her way to the bedroom, removed her riding clothes, and fell sound asleep on top of the quilt.

DRU KNOCKED at room 212. Impatient, he knocked louder.

"Hold your horses," a drowsy voice called out. "If this is you, Christian, I'm going to thump your head."

The door was yanked open, and Dru stood facing his older brother.

"What do you want?" Freddy asked with a surly tone.

"We need to talk."

"Wrong. You need to talk. I don't have anything to say to you. Now, I've got to be up at five in the morning. I need my sleep. How about hitting the road?"

Dru started to push his way inside his brother's room, but he didn't. Instead he stood in the motel doorway staring at his brother, searching hard for the young boy he had vague memories of—the one who had helped him tie his roller skates and taught him to ride a bicycle without training wheels.

"What's wrong with you?" Freddy asked. "You're looking at me like you see a ghost."

"Maybe I do," Dru said. For the first time in many years, he was able to see the boy who'd once been his brother.

"Freddy, what happened in the summer of 1975?" Dru asked, as unprepared for the question as Freddy was.

"What's wrong with you?" Freddy countered.

"May I come in?"

Freddy stepped back. "Sure, help yourself. Saying no wouldn't do any good, would it? You're the law. I'm a convicted felon. Saying no to the law isn't part of my rights any longer. And before you bother to check, I'm on parole. My officer in Jackson knows I'm here in Natchez working this job. Everything is copacetic."

"I know. I've already checked."

A flush of anger touched Freddy's cheeks. "You *are* just like the old man. You see me and immediately assume I'm in trouble somewhere. He never gave me the benefit of the doubt and you're following in his footsteps."

Dru heard the heartbreak behind the anger for the first time. He'd never stopped to consider how hard it had been on Freddy to always be the one the finger of blame pointed out. And there was some truth to his brother's complaints. By the time Freddy left home, whenever there was trouble in town, the first assumption was that Freddy was somehow involved.

"I'm sorry," Dru said. "I was doing my job."

"Do you know how many times I heard that?"

"Too many." Dru pushed on. "I need your help, Freddy. Things are happening up at Blackthorn."

"Oh, right. Here it comes. Someone is stealing something and I'm the perfect suspect. Hey, it's probably Freddy. Everyone knows he's a thief. Remember the time he stole that pocketknife from the dime store or the shoe strings from the boot shop? Yeah, he's been on a crime spree since he was twelve."

Dru didn't try to stop him or interrupt. Freddy was angry, but he was also in pain. And perhaps the best thing for him to do would be to vent his pain.

"Aren't you going to deny it?" Freddy asked.

"I didn't come here to question you about the burglaries. I came to ask for your help." He was gratified by the look of surprise on his brother's face.

"How can I help you?"

"Tell me about the summer of 1975," Dru said.

Turning away, Freddy shrugged. "It was hot."

But Dru had seen something in his brother's eyes. Something he'd never expected to see. Fear. It had slipped up and shown itself before Freddy could turn away.

"Something terrible happened, didn't it?" he pressed.

"Yeah, Mom died."

"Something else."

"Wasn't that bad enough? Mom died and Dad turned into this stranger who blamed me for everything that went wrong in town."

"What happened?" Dru asked again.

"How old were you that summer?" Freddy asked unexpectedly.

"Nine."

"Right. I remember. You'd just started playing Little League and were a damn fine catcher."

Dru felt again the blush at his older brother's praise. They'd spent many long, hot afternoons practicing. Freddy had shown him how to catch, and how to bat. He'd taught him to be tough and fair.

"I was good because you took the time to show me."

"Yeah. We spent some hours working on it. After Mom died it seemed best to keep you busy."

"Thanks, Freddy. Maybe I never said it, but baseball saved me that summer."

Freddy paced the room. "Dru, I need to get some sleep. We have an early call. We're going to be doing the ornamental trim on the second-floor windows. That's my specialty and I need to be on top of things."

"Why won't you tell me about the summer?"

"Because sometimes the past is better left alone. I buried my ghosts, Dru. I don't need to go digging things up."

REBECCA FOUGHT her way out of a deep sleep to semi-wakefulness, aware that her heart was pounding. Someone was in the room with her. She knew it even as she ignored her screaming ribs and sat up in the bed.

Shadows filled the corners of the room, and she searched carefully, stopping at the darkest corner where the half-open door created a thick, black shadow against the wall. Someone was there. She knew it.

The blood roared in her ears. There wasn't a single thing that would serve as a weapon in the bedroom. Not even a book she could throw.

The pain in her ribs was severe enough that she wanted to cry out, but she didn't.

"Who are you?" she asked, aware that in her need for sleep she hadn't bothered to put on a nightshirt. She reached down and picked up her shirt where she'd dropped it on the floor and slipped into it.

The person standing behind the door didn't answer.

"What do you want from me?" she asked again. This time her voice was stronger. She took some courage from that.

For one instant she thought she might have been imagining that someone else was in the room. Maybe it was just one of those eerie dreams where she'd imagined someone standing over her, staring down at her.

"Get off Blackthorn land," a male voice said from behind the door.

Rebecca felt her heart surge with fear. She thought for a moment she might faint, but she concentrated on breathing. "What is it you want?" she asked again.

"Leave here. Stop now and just leave."

"Why?"

"I can't tell you. If you go now, no one else will be hurt."

"Who are you?" Rebecca asked.

"It doesn't matter who I am. Leave and stay away. Don't dig up the Indian mound anymore."

"If we don't explore the mound, someone else will."

"That's not your concern," the man said. "Leave now. I only came to warn you. If you don't want to be hurt again, go away."

The door moved and in the dim moonlight that filtered through the window, Rebecca saw a man of average height and slender build slip out from behind the door and leave. She was still sitting in bed when she heard the exterior door of the cottage snap shut.

DRU HEARD the ringing of the telephone and reached across the pillow for it. He wasn't certain if he was dreaming or if the sound was real, but he answered.

"Colson, this is Brett. You'd better get up here to Blackthorn. Someone broke into the cottage and scared Rebecca half to death."

"Rebecca's in the hospital," he said, wondering what kind of idiotic joke Brett was trying to pull.

"Think again. If you doubt me, give the hospital a call. She made an escape and came back to Blackthorn."

"Is she hurt?" Dru was wide awake. He should have known better than to trust that Rebecca would do as she'd been told.

"No, but she's pretty badly shaken up. She asked me to call you. The phone in the cottage is out so I'm on a cell," Brett explained.

"I'm on my way," Dru said, searching in the darkness for his clothes.

As he drove, he reassured himself with Brett's promise that Rebecca was only scared. Someone had broken into her cottage. As soon as he got the story straight, he'd have a forensic team in there and this time, maybe, they'd find some clues.

He wasn't surprised when he got to Blackthorn to see that the entire camp was on alert. Brett and Regina sat in front of a campfire with Rebecca. In the glow of the fire, she was beautiful. It was only when she lifted her gaze to his as he walked up that he saw how truly haunted she was. Someone had frightened her, and badly.

"Rebecca." He knelt beside her and scooped her into his arms, holding her lightly, remembering her ribs. "Did he hurt you?"

"No," she said, and her voice was tightly controlled. "He didn't try to hurt me. He warned me. He told me to stop the construction and the dig and to leave Blackthorn."

Dru felt her body tremble and he rubbed her back lightly. "Was it the same person who attacked you in the woods?" he asked.

"I don't know," she said. "It could have been, but I don't know. I didn't see him tonight. I only know it was a man because of his voice."

Dru soothed her. When he could feel the tense muscles in her back begin to relax a little, he spoke softly in her ear. "I'm going to call in some deputies to go over the cottage. We need to find out how he got in. Are you okay with Brett and Regina?"

"Sure," she said, forcing her voice to be strong. Dru had never admired her more. "I'm actually okay. He just frightened me, and I guess since I was already hurt, I felt a little more vulnerable."

"I'd say you had a right to feel vulnerable," Regina said. "Whoever is doing this has to be caught and punished. I don't understand how he can slip by guards and all of us and just come and go as he pleases."

"It's obviously someone who knows Blackthorn a lot better than any of us," Dru said. That finger of blame pointed squarely at Randall Levert. No wonder he couldn't find Randall at the car lot or his home. He was likely already on the premises of Blackthorn and planning his strategic attack on Rebecca.

Dru wanted to talk to Rebecca alone. He needed to. He had to tell her about Freddy and his growing suspicions about the past. But he wanted to talk to her privately and now wasn't a good time. Standing up, he asked her gently if she wanted to go and stay with Joey.

"Yes," she said, allowing Dru to help her to her feet. "I feel exhausted."

"I don't suppose it would do any good to point out to you that you should have stayed in the hospital," Dru said dryly.

"Hindsight is always twenty-twenty."

He smiled at the hint of spirit that had returned to her voice. That was a good sign. He glanced over his shoulder at Brett. "Please ask everyone to remain in the campsite area. Forensics will go over the cottage and then my deputies will need to question everyone. If there's the slightest chance anyone saw anything, we need to find out about it."

"Do you think the attack on Rebecca is linked to the person who stole the Black Stick?" Brett asked hopefully.

"Possibly," Dru said. "We'll know more after we investigate."

# CHAPTER FIFTEEN

"I'M ABSOLUTELY FINE," Rebecca reassured Joey as she settled on the sofa with Dru. She sipped the bourbon Dru had poured for her. She'd left the hospital without even an aspirin for pain.

"Are you gonna catch the man who scared her?" Joey asked Dru.

"You bet." He gave Rebecca's hand a gentle squeeze.

"Rebecca, you should stay here with me so I can look out for you," Joey said.

"I think I'll do just that," Rebecca said, squeezing Dru's hand in return.

"And I'll go do some investigating now that I know Rebecca's safe," Dru said.

"Good. Then I'm going back to bed. I have fruit trees to plant tomorrow. It'll be a small orchard, but it's something Aurelia really wanted."

"We're fine down here," Rebecca assured Joey as he climbed the stairs to his bedroom. "See you in the morning."

When he was gone, Rebecca leaned against Dru's chest. "Thanks for not upsetting him. All of this has been hard on Joey. He was so worried earlier today that I was injured. Now this." She sighed.

"This won't go on much longer. We're going to catch whoever did this and put a stop to it."

"I know you will," she whispered against his chest. He was so solid, so strong. And she had no doubt that Dru would prevail. He wasn't the kind of man who accepted anything less than success.

"Do you think you'd recognize the man's voice again if you heard it?"

That was a question Rebecca had already asked herself. She'd been so frightened. The voice had been so calm, so ordinary. Was it possible she'd heard it correctly? "I'm not sure," she admitted. "I was so scared."

"It's okay," Dru assured her, rubbing her back gently. "I'm going to bring you a tape recording we made during Aurelia's trial, and I want you to listen to it. If you can match the voice to the man who broke into the cottage, that'll be good. If you can't, we'll find another way to identify him. Believe me, he's going to make a mistake."

"I have to be certain," Rebecca said.

"And I want you to be sure." Dru had never been one to go forward with a half-hearted eyewitness. He'd learned through the years that even an eyewitness who was absolutely positive of what he'd seen could be wrong.

"Why is someone doing this?" Rebecca asked. Leaning against Dru she felt strong enough to consider the possibilities.

"If we had a clear-cut motive, we'd be a lot further down the road of figuring out who is doing this," Dru said. "I suspect Randall Levert, but what reason does he have? He could jeopardize his parole and end up back in jail just for setting foot on Blackthorn property. Why? What could possibly motivate him to risk so much?"

"Is he stable enough to think this through?" Rebecca asked.

"That's the wild card. Randall could just have stepped off the deep end. His obsession with Blackthorn might be at the root of everything."

"But you aren't certain it's Randall Levert?" Rebecca knew Dru well enough to sense his hesitation. He wanted to believe it was Randall, but there wasn't enough proof.

"I hate to admit it, but John Ittawasa could also be right. This might be targeted at preventing the exploration of the burial mound."

"Why?" Rebecca was surprised.

"Bigotry or even some form of religious belief that graves shouldn't be disturbed. Who knows? I'm just saying it's a possibility."

"I still haven't spoken with John," she admitted. "I tried to call him tonight, but the phone lines were down at the cottage. I have to admit, I was relieved. At least until I needed a telephone and had to run through the darkness to get Brett."

"I'll take care of the phone lines," Dru said. "And I'm getting you a cell phone first thing in the morning."

"Don't worry. I've already thought of that."

"Now sip your drink, ease back on the pillows, and let me get that blanket Joey left for you. You need to sleep," Dru told her.

Rebecca let him lift her feet and ease them up on the sofa. When he covered her with the soft blanket, she snuggled into it. "This is wonderful."

"Rebecca, I have to tell you something. My older brother Freddy is working here at Blackthorn."

"I know," she said. "Joey pointed him out to me. Why didn't you tell me your brother was working here?"

"I didn't know at first." Dru shook his head. "Our relationship is...difficult. But I was talking with Freddy last night. He's had some trouble with the law in the past, but I don't believe he's involved in this. However, I'm not ruling anyone or anything out until we have this resolved."

"Thank you, Dru." She felt as if her body weighed a thousand pounds. Even her eyelids were heavy.

"I've got work to do, Rebecca. Will you be okay?"

"I'll be fine." She touched his cheek. The stubble of his beard was rough. She ran her hand down his cheek, amazed that even through her exhaustion and the lethargy left in the wake of extreme fear, she also felt desire. Love was a strange and wonderful thing. It was there, beneath every other emotion.

Sitting on the edge of the sofa, Dru leaned down and

brushed his lips over hers, a feathery kiss that made her body tingle for something more substantial.

"I want to make love to you," Dru whispered.

The words were like an electric touch. "I know," she answered. "I forget everything else when you touch me."

He kissed her again, this time with passion.

Rebecca felt her body respond. Even the warning signal of pain from her ribs was inconsequential as she put her arms around his neck and pulled herself against him.

Dru kissed her with thoroughness and then gently pulled back. "You get some rest. When we finally have some time to be alone, I want you completely fresh."

He was right. She didn't like it, but she knew it. Smiling up at him, she touched his lips with her finger. "I'll take a rain check on this, but only because I don't have a choice."

"You rest. I'll be back later and I'll tell you everything I found out. And I'll talk to John. In fact, I'm going to need his help."

"Thanks, Dru," she said. Her eyelids were suddenly heavy again. Intoxicated with Dru, she'd forgotten how tired she was.

"Sleep," he whispered, pulling the blanket up to her chin. "Sleep," he said even more softly as he stood up and left her, hair fanned over the pillow on Joey's sofa.

DRU POUNDED harder on Randall Levert's door. He saw a light come on in the neighbor's house and he didn't care.

"Levert," he said, "open the door now."

The neighbor's window slid up and a frightened voice called into the fading night. "I'm calling the law."

"Don't bother," Dru said. "I'm a law officer. I'm here to see Randall Levert."

"Good luck," the neighbor said. "He's never at home. He comes in for five minutes and then rushes back out. And he used to be such a nice, neat neighbor."

Dru knew he had to accept that Randall wasn't at home. It was frustrating, but he couldn't change it. Instead, he walked over to the neighbor's window.

"When was the last time you saw Mr. Levert?" he asked.

"I couldn't say," the neighbor said. "By the way, I'm Barnaby Lomis."

"Sheriff Dru Colson," Dru said, holding up his identification to the window. "You're Randall's neighbor. Surely you've seen him in the past week?"

"Have you seen his yard? It's a total mess. And the man can afford a lawn service if he doesn't want to do it himself. Brings the whole neighborhood down. When his mother was alive, she'd never let things get into such a state. Still, I guess I should be patient with him. Maybe he's going through some kind of grieving phase."

"Mr. Lomis, think hard. Did you see Randall out getting his newspaper, maybe? Or watering his lawn?"

"Nope. He's keeping very strange hours. He used to get the paper at the crack of dawn. Then he'd leave at seven sharp for the car lot. Now, sometimes that paper lies on the front lawn until dusk. Then it's gone, like he slips out of the house as soon as it's dark and gets it. Like he doesn't want anyone to see him. I guess he's ashamed of all that stuff he got into earlier when his mother was killed!" Barnaby widened his eyes in mock horror.

Dru found that the talkative Barnaby Lomis was getting on his last nerve. The man loved the sound of his own voice though he had little to contribute.

"Have you seen anyone else at Randall's house?" Dru asked. He didn't expect to hear anything useful, but it was a routine question.

Barnaby Lomis's face turned thoughtful. "Funny you should ask that. There *has* been a strange person at his house."

"Really," Dru said, wondering if he could believe Lomis. "Can you describe this person?"

"Yes. Very well." Lomis sniffed, as if he found Dru's skepticism offensive. "Average height, slender, short dark hair, quick-moving. Very agile. Dark in that Goth sort of way, like those young kids who want to be vampires. If you ask me, they should be given psychiatric help. They're—"

"Please, just describe the person you saw. Was it a man or a woman?"

"Could've been a slender man or a tall woman. Can't say for certain. Drove a dark sedan. Can't be sure of the type of car. Those kinds of things don't interest me."

Dru made a mental note of everything Lomis said. He was surprisingly good with his memory of detail. "Why did you notice this person?" he asked.

"Really! You should have to ask! The house is shut

up like a morgue for months and suddenly this caller shows up two or three times a week at very irregular hours."

"When was the last time you saw this visitor?"

"Oh, that would have been Friday afternoon, around three o'clock. I remember the time specifically, because I thought Randall was gone. But the visitor went to the house and never came back, so I can only assume he got in. There's a holly hedge that blocks my view of the back door, so I can't say for certain what really happened."

"Thank you, Mr. Lomis, for your extensive observations and acute eye for the details of the lives of others," Dru said, knowing the sarcasm would be totally wasted. What Dru had learned was that Lomis referred to the visitor as a he. In Lomis's mind, he'd assigned a sex to the person.

"Any time," Barnaby Lomis said.

Dru checked his watch. It was five o'clock. Dawn would be breaking soon and he'd had very little sleep. If he wouldn't disturb Rebecca, he'd go back to Joey's, just to be there and watch over her. She'd be sound asleep by now, though, and it was best to leave her to her rest. She needed as much sleep as she could get to heal properly.

The case was at a momentary lull. He decided to go home and capitalize on the downtime. He, too, would function better with some rest. By morning, the forensic team would be ready to give him a report on the break-in at the cottage. And maybe in the daylight he could run down the elusive Randall Levert.

BRIGHT SUNLIGHT and the smell of coffee awoke Rebecca. For a moment she was completely disoriented. She had no idea where she was or who was making the sounds of breakfast.

"One sugar or two?" Joey asked as he came around the corner and smiled at her.

"No sugar, just black," she said, starting to swing her feet to the floor. A stabbing pain in her torso stopped her. She'd forgotten about her ribs, too.

"I made some toast," Joey said. "I wanted to make a real breakfast, but I'm not sure how."

"Toast is perfect," she said, easing to her feet. She was still wearing her riding clothes from the day before. It was a toss-up which she wanted more—that cup of coffee or a shower.

"You had a visitor early this morning. Mr. Ittawasa came by. He said not to wake you."

"What time is it?" She was startled, and a little panicked by the thought of John Ittawasa. He would be furious—and rightly so—about the loss of the Black Stick.

"It's a little after ten."

"You let me sleep half the morning away," she accused Joey. "You should have gotten me up."

"Right. A volcano couldn't have gotten you up. You were exhausted. Dru said to let you sleep."

"Was he here, too?" she asked.

"Twice. He's down at the cottage, I think."

"Can I take a rain check on the toast, Joey?"

He shook his head. "You should always eat breakfast. You told me that yourself."

Hoist with her own petard. She walked into the kitchen and took a slice of toast from the dish he'd prepared. "I'll eat it on my way," she said, refilling her coffee cup. "And I'll drink, too."

"Tell Dru the coffee's made when he wants some."

"I will." She hurried outside, blinking at the brightness of the day. Even though her ribs hurt, she felt much better than she had the evening before. She was on the mend.

Passing the construction site, she saw the men there hard at it. Dru's brother, Freddy, stood in the window waiting for some material to be lifted up to him. She had the feeling he was watching her, yet when she waved up at him, he turned and stepped away from the window, disappearing from sight.

She saw Dru's official car in front of the cottage and was glad she'd managed to avoid Brett and the other members of his team on the way down.

Dru was inside the cottage with two deputies. They were talking, one deputy pointing to the front door. "There was no sign of forced entry, Dru. Either he had a key or she left the door unlocked."

Rebecca stopped on the porch, but Dru had already seen her.

"I may have been so exhausted that I left the door unlocked," Rebecca said.

"So he could have gotten inside the cottage and waited for you to return?" the deputy asked.

"That's right." She felt more than foolish. "I won't be that careless again."

Dru signaled her inside. "We found lots of fingerprints, but most of them will be yours and Aurelia's, Joey's, Marcus's…" he shrugged. "The best lead we have is your ability to recognize this guy's voice."

"I'll do my best." She was feeling less and less capable of identifying anything or anyone.

"Good. Sit down," Dru said, pointing to the kitchen table where a tape recorder had already been set up. "This is a tape I made this year. Just listen to it, okay?"

"Sure." She eyed the machine dubiously.

He sat across from her while the two deputies remained standing but listened carefully.

Dru pressed the play button and the cassette slowly started to wind through the machine.

*The last time I saw my mother was when she was telling me that she'd been threatened by Aurelia Agee. Mother insisted that Aurelia was concerned about her claim to be heir to Blackthorn. She said Aurelia physically assaulted her, and then said she would do worse if Mother didn't drop her claim.*

Rebecca listened to the voice in total fascination. There was the same quiet cadence, the bass note of depressed acceptance.

"That's him," she said without hesitation.

"Are you positive?" Dru asked.

"As positive as I can be. It sounds just like him. So quiet. I mean he was different last night. He was more…

keyed up. Actually, he sounded a little desperate last night. Like he didn't know what he was going to do if I didn't take his warning seriously."

"Listen a little more," Dru suggested.

He played another two minutes of the tape before Rebecca signaled him to stop. "That's the same man who was in this cottage last night. I can only presume from the content of the tape that it's Randall Levert."

"None other," Dru said grimly.

"Have you talked to Randall?" she asked.

"No, I haven't," Dru said. "I can't find him. I've been hunting him for two days."

"The car lot's been closed all week," one of the deputies said. "My wife wanted to buy a truck. She went down there four or five times and never did catch anyone there. I heard he fired all of his salespeople."

"Same story I heard." Dru rewound the tape and stood up. "I'm very interested in finding Randall. Lee, you take the car lot and Rick, you take his house. Stake it out. And if you see him, call me before you do anything."

"You've got it, Sheriff," Rick said as Lee nodded. The two deputies went out together.

"What is it?" Rebecca asked. She didn't like the worried look on Dru's face.

"It's Randall. It just isn't like him to disappear like this."

"He hasn't disappeared," Rebecca pointed out. "He may not be at work or home, but he's been here. At Blackthorn, paying visits to me."

"Randall's a foolish man, obviously. But I never thought he was so stupid. There's just something about all of this that doesn't feel right to me."

"What?" Rebecca asked.

"I'm just not certain. Yet."

## CHAPTER SIXTEEN

REBECCA LEFT Dru organizing a search of Blackthorn woods. She accepted the cell phone he insisted that she take and walked back to the dig site where Brett and his crew were continuing with the excavation.

She watched for a little while, her anxiety growing. She signaled Brett over when he took a break.

"Maybe we should halt the dig for a few days," she said. She'd been thinking it over, and she was certain John Ittawasa was going to demand that all excavation be stopped. She wouldn't blame him. She'd lost one of the most valuable artifacts in the history of Mississippi Indians. It would be better for all if she stopped the excavation before John had to ask.

"I'm not stopping," Brett said point-blank. "I'm not responsible for what happened, and I won't be punished. We're making major discoveries and just because you didn't do your job is no reason to stop me from doing mine."

She looked at him. Brett had a lot of problems, and she wasn't in the mood to mollycoddle him. "This isn't all about you," she said, having to work to keep her voice even. "This is about—"

"Let the dig continue."

She turned around to face John Ittawasa. She hadn't heard him come up the makeshift steps, but he was standing right behind her.

"John, I don't know what to say. I'm totally responsible for the loss of the Black Stick." She stared into his dark eyes. "I promised you I would take it to the vault and I didn't. There's nothing I can do to make up for what happened."

"Perhaps you should have taken the Stick to the vault as you promised, but you didn't steal it. Someone else did that. It's my conclusion that you were attacked to draw attention away from the artifact so that it could be stolen." He glanced at Brett. "Leaving it unprotected was your decision, Mr. Gibson, not Ms. Barrett's. While I understand your concern for her safety when her horse came back riderless, the relic was still in your possession and therefore your responsibility."

Rebecca held her breath, waiting for Brett to blow a gasket. He wasn't a man who took criticism with grace, and John had completely turned the tables of blame around on him.

"I think that's hogwash. Rebecca said she'd handle it. She went off to ride that stupid horse instead of taking it to the bank. You can't lay this at my door." Brett's cheeks were flushed with anger and his eyes sparkled.

"Of course I can," John said, unperturbed. "It's my understanding that you delayed the transfer of the relic because you wanted to photograph it to document the find."

Rebecca saw the truth hit home with Brett, and she then saw him begin to deflect it. She stepped forward. "The truth is, it doesn't matter what happened yesterday. We can't change that. We have to concentrate on today and the best way to protect the history of the Mound Builders."

"And I believe the best way to do that is to find the person who stole the artifact. To do that, we need to continue the dig," John said. "Only if he believes we won't be stopped and that we'll turn up other valuable artifacts will he attempt to strike again."

Rebecca looked from John to Brett and saw the surprise on the dig director's face. He was as startled by John's turnaround as she was.

"I believe the worst thing that can happen would be to stop now," John said. "I've talked this over with Dru. If the intent of the burglar is to stop the dig to prevent the exploration of the mound, then that's exactly what we must not do. But I want several of my men at the dig site and at least three more guarding any additional relics that are discovered."

Rebecca glanced at Brett and was further surprised to see that he wasn't going to raise any objections.

"We want to preserve our find as much as anyone else," Brett said. "My reputation is at stake, and that may not seem as important to you as what we discover, but I can assure you it's of vital importance to me."

John's smile was slow. "Your point is well taken, Mr. Gibson. Then we're in agreement."

"Agreement about what?" Regina asked as she walked up.

"We're going forward," Brett said, giving her arm a light squeeze. "Now let's get to work. We're at a level where I think we're really going to begin to turn up some interesting things."

Brett was in an expansive mood, and he turned back to John. "The reason we believe the Black Stick was so close to the surface is that it was a ceremonial element of the burial. Because the tribe was in decline, the symbol of leadership was placed closer to the surface instead of with the body of the king. That would allow the successor to find the scepter and assume the rule without disturbing the entire mound."

"That goes with the legends of my people," John said. "The king was a wise leader. He knew that the days of the Mound Builders were limited. His son was killed in battle, but there was a nephew, a very young boy at the time, who was next in the line of succession. He would have made it as easy as possible for Kilana to rule."

"Yes," Brett said with some excitement. "That fits perfectly with the theory I was developing. As we move deeper into the mound, we'll begin to find the items that tell the personal history of the king."

"Exactly," John said.

"What about the burglaries?" Regina asked, interrupting the conversation. "What if we find something else really important and it's stolen?"

"There won't be any more burglaries," John said flatly. "And we will recover what was stolen. Dru is working on it, and so am I. The culprit will be found and punished and the Black Stick and the stolen bowl will be restored."

Regina nodded, her blond ponytail bobbing. "I just spoke to my dad, and he's going to put up some guards at the construction site. He's afraid that someone may try to sabotage his equipment."

"I think every precaution we take in the future is to our advantage," Rebecca said. "I'll speak with Eugene and Roy."

"Any idea who broke into your cottage?" Regina asked. "I heard you left the door unlocked."

Rebecca was unsettled, but she realized that Regina was a young woman slightly spoiled and more than a little presumptuous. "Dru is following several leads," she said vaguely.

"Dru's organizing a search of the property," Regina continued. "Does he think the person is still on the premises?"

"You'd have to ask Dru what he thinks." Rebecca turned to Brett. "Whatever you find, take it instantly to the bank vault, okay?"

"You got it," Brett said.

"I'll escort you to talk with the sheriff," John said, taking Rebecca's elbow. "We need to coordinate our efforts in all of this."

"Are we going to help with the search?" Regina asked, unwilling to let it go. "I've never been on a man-hunt. Dru must think that someone is still on Blackthorn property. This is too cool."

"I think you'd be more useful here, helping Brett," John said before Rebecca could answer. He exerted the lightest pressure on Rebecca's arm and directed her toward the steps that led down the mound.

When they were at the bottom, he turned a worried gaze to her. "I'm deeply upset, but I think it important to show a united front here."

"I agree," Rebecca said. She wanted to thank John but she wasn't sure how to do it. "We will get to the bottom of this, John. I'll do whatever I can to make up for what's happened here, and no matter what you said to Brett, I hold myself totally responsible."

"Our goal is to find the thief. We don't have a choice now. That artifact must be returned. It's part of our heritage. The markings on that relic will tell many things about my people."

"Brett did take numerous photographs," Rebecca said, knowing it was a poor substitute for the relic.

"That, at least, is some minor consolation. But let's focus on the search. Dru is bringing in his deputy with the dog. My men will work with his. This person who broke into your cottage last night must be found."

There was a grimness in John's voice that Rebecca had never heard before.

"I'm sure Dru will find him."

"Yes, and when he does, he'll tell us exactly what he's done with those stolen items."

DRU SPREAD the deputies and volunteers in a thin line. They were within hailing distance of each other but covering as much ground as possible. Press and his dog were in the lead with several of John Ittawasa's best trackers. He'd requested help from volunteers from sheriff's departments in surrounding counties and was expecting reinforcements after lunch.

Now, though, he was pushing forward. He'd managed a match on fingerprints found in Rebecca's cottage. Randall Levert had been in Rebecca's bedroom. He'd touched the door, most likely pulling it back so that he had a place to hide while she got ready for bed.

The idea of it scalded Dru. Randall could have hurt Rebecca. He could have done the unthinkable—he could have killed her.

He was bumped from his thoughts when Joey walked up leading the two horses. "Cogar is saddled, too. I'll go get him. Mariah is fine," Joey said, pointing to the stitches in her shoulder, "as long as you don't get her hot."

"Not a problem," Dru said.

"And stay on the trail. Don't go into the woods where something could tear them out."

Dru hid his smile. No horse could have a better protector than Joey. He was determined to make sure Mariah, Cogar and Diable got only the best treatment.

"Rebecca is going to ride Mariah, and I assure you, she'll be treated with kid gloves."

"Okay," Joey said, but he was still reluctant about handing over the horses. "Check the girths and be sure they're tight. Cogar likes to blow up a little."

"Thanks, Joey," Dru said, "and remember your promise."

"I'm going over to the construction site now. But I've got those fruit trees and their roots are drying out. I should be planting them."

"You promised," Dru said. He had to be certain Joey would be with the construction crew instead of alone in the gardens. Dru couldn't risk that Randall would happen on Joey and hurt him or take him hostage. Once upon a time, Dru would never have believed Randall capable of violence. Now he wasn't certain what Randall was capable of.

He saw Rebecca and John walking down the drive and he felt a rush of concern for Rebecca. She insisted she was fine, but he could see the faint etching of pain in her face. He'd been torn when she insisted on joining the search, and he'd finally compromised when she'd suggested she ride instead of walk.

As she approached the horses, she went straight to Mariah and examined her neck where the fine stitches marred her beautiful golden skin.

"Joey said someone deliberately hurt her," Rebecca said, angrier at the injury to the horse than her own.

"It looked like the horse charged into the woods. She must have startled the person attacking you and they struck out at her with the same weapon they'd been using to hit you," Dru said.

"Mariah went into the woods to protect Rebecca," Joey said stoutly. "She knew someone was hurting Rebecca and she went to help."

"She's a very noble animal," John said, nodding to Joey. "I believe you're right. She went to protect Ms. Barrett."

"I'll be very easy with her," Rebecca promised as she allowed Dru to give her a lift into the saddle.

Dru saw the pain shift across her face but he kept his comments to himself. If she was determined to ride, there was no stopping her.

"Let's ride," John said, swinging into the saddle on Diable's back. "I love this animal."

Dru mounted and the three of them headed toward the winding trail that would take them by the burial mound and the thicket of devil's walking stick for which Blackthorn had been named. It was already late afternoon, and Dru had a feeling that the day was going to become even more eventful.

REBECCA IGNORED the jarring pain in her ribs, forced herself to sit up taller and relax in the saddle. Now the motion was gentle, rhythmic and soothing. She just had to sit tall to protect her injured body.

To her right the men were moving through the thicket. The dog had yet to pick up a scent, but there was an air of expectancy. It was both exciting and frightening.

Dru had shared his theory about Randall Levert with her, and the matching fingerprints seemed to confirm it. But Rebecca was troubled. The man who'd hidden in her cottage had to be delivering a warning rather than a threat. Of course, in the dead of night she'd felt awfully threatened. But, looking back over the event, she'd come to see what had transpired in a different light.

Randall had made no attempt to touch her. He'd simply warned her to halt the dig and leave Blackthorn. But why? What would he gain from stopping the dig and forcing her to leave?

"Are you hurting?" Dru asked, edging closer to her so that he could speak softly.

She smiled. "I'm thinking. Maybe that's painful."

He touched her knee and she felt a sizzle that moved up her thigh. Dru ignited her passion. There was no other way to explain her reaction to his slightest touch.

"We'll get to the bottom of this," Dru assured her.

"What could Randall possibly gain by stopping the dig and frightening us all away?" she asked. "That's what I'm trying to figure out."

Dru shook his head. "I don't think rational thought will work here. Randall's gone round the bend, I'm afraid. Blackthorn has become an obsession with him. It's as if he can't let it go."

"But he was so specific last night. He wanted us to *stop digging* and leave. Why not just tell us to leave?"

"We'll have to ask him when we find him," Dru said. "Until then, don't worry about it. There's no way to figure out what he's thinking. Believe me, I've tried."

"And the whole baby thing. What's that about?" Rebecca persisted.

Dru shook his head. "Randall is sick. It's going to take a team of psychiatrists to figure out what's going on in his head. I have to admit, though, the crying baby intrigues me. It's become a theme with him."

"Listen!" John held up a hand to halt them.

They stopped their horses and listened. The dog had picked up a scent. It was baying loudly and with great excitement. There was also a cry from Press.

"We're on the trail," John said with some eagerness. "It sounds like they're driving him straight into our arms."

Dru unclipped the holster at his side. John, too, reached into his coat and removed a pistol. Rebecca looked at the weapons with dread.

"Don't hurt him," she said, realizing that somewhere along the trail her fear of Randall Levert had turned into sympathy. "If he's sick, he can't help himself."

"We won't hurt him unless we have to," Dru assured her.

"We want him alive so he can tell us where he put the stolen items," John said.

"Rebecca, maybe you should ride back," Dru suggested.

She shook her head. "Not on your life, Sheriff. I've come this far. I'm going to see it through."

"Okay," he said, dismounting. He walked over and helped her to the ground. "Will you hold the horses while John and I angle through the woods? You have the cell phone I gave you in case you see or hear anything."

She took the reins and in doing so touched his hand. "Be careful," she whispered.

He brushed a kiss across her lips. "I'll be back before long."

She watched the two men ease into the underbrush. The hound was baying frantically and now she could hear the voices of some of the men. They seemed on a hot, fresh trail, and they were covering the ground fast. At the pace they were going, it wouldn't take Dru and John long to get to the dog.

She looked into the dense woods and imagined Randall Levert fleeing before the dog and men. He would be terrified, she was sure, and she felt again the strange pity.

Loud yells came from some of the men. She felt a tremor pass through Mariah and turned her attention to soothing the restless horses. They'd picked up on the excitement and were becoming antsy. Talking softly to the horses, she tried to make out what was happening in the woods. The men sounded only a hundred or so yards away, but it was difficult to tell distance through the dense trees and underbrush.

"Stand back!"

She clearly heard Dru's voice, and then a curse from John Ittawasa. She knew then that something dreadful had happened.

She shifted her position so she could see better. When one of the deputies came out of the woods and walked up to her, she forced her voice to be calm, level.

"What happened?" she asked.

"The sheriff told me to hold the horses so you could go in," he said, reaching for the reins.

"What happened?" she asked, wanting a little time to prepare herself for what she'd begun to suspect would be a gruesome scene.

"It's the suspect, Randall Levert," the deputy said. "He's dead, ma'am. Looks like he was stabbed to death and left in the woods. The sheriff needs you to look at some evidence."

# CHAPTER SEVENTEEN

DRU KNELT BESIDE Randall's body as one of the deputies put plastic gloves over his hands to preserve any evidence that might be there. He felt a keen sense of duty to uncover Randall's killer. He'd never expected to find the car salesman dead.

"Sheriff," the deputy said.

"Yes?" Dru tore his gaze away from Randall's terrified face.

"He's got something in his hand. It looks like one of those little knit socks that a baby would wear," the deputy said.

That's when Dru had sent for Rebecca. As much as he hated for her to see the body, he needed to know if the bootee in Randall's hand matched the one she'd found in the woods. It looked the same to him, but Rebecca had studied the ribbon and lace edging of the bootee.

He saw her approaching and felt a lull in the dark emotions that always came with a murder case. Rebecca was the antithesis of darkness. She was light and hope and kindness. She came straight to the body, determined to do whatever was necessary. She made him proud. She was a woman with unique courage.

"Poor Randall," she said, standing at the edge of the scene. "The deputy said he was stabbed."

"That's the initial finding. We'll know for certain when the autopsy is complete."

"Something really frightened him." Rebecca turned away. "It's ironic that only a few hours ago he was frightening me. Now he's dead."

Dru pointed to Randall's clenched fist where part of the baby bootee protruded. "It looks like this bootee is a match to the one you found. Can you say for sure?" he asked.

Rebecca knelt down and examined the tiny garment. She didn't touch it but she examined the edging of lace and the pink ribbon woven through the material.

"It looks exactly like it," she said, "but they all sort of look alike. I'd have to see them side by side."

"We'll match it for certain at the office."

"What now?" Rebecca asked.

"We continue with the search," Dru said grimly. "Whoever killed Randall was on Blackthorn property, and he may still be here." He called the men around him.

"Press, can your dog pick up a new scent here?"

"Sure thing. In fact he's on one now. It heads due north."

John Ittawasa touched Dru's arm. "I have five men posted on the north side of the property. If anyone tries to leave Blackthorn from that route, he'll be caught."

Dru nodded his thanks. "This has become a hot trail. I'll call for reinforcements on the south and east. The only way to escape on the west is the river, and that's been covered for several days. If the killer is still in here, we're tightening the net. Now everybody stay alert."

He sent most of the men through the woods with Press and the dog leading the way. He held back five men. "Retrace your steps," he told them, "and meet us at the dig site. Check with Billy down at that narrow landing on the river and make sure he hasn't seen anything." He turned to the tallest deputy. "Jason, you wait here with the body until the coroner comes and removes it."

"Yes, sir," the deputy said. "Any special instructions for him?"

"We need the coroner's findings as soon as possible."

"Do you really think the killer is still around here?" Rebecca asked when Jason got on the radio. The other men had departed and she felt comfortable voicing her fear in front of Dru and John.

"There's a good probability. Let's go."

"What's our assignment?" John asked.

"Press can handle the search through the woods," Dru said. "We're going back to the dig. This isn't burglary anymore. It's murder. And everyone is a suspect."

"You mean Brett, don't you?" Rebecca asked. It wasn't surprising. Brett's behavior was so aggressive, his anger so excessive. He made a perfect murder suspect. "He's a handful, but I still don't see him as a murderer," she said.

"Maybe, maybe not."

Dru was interrupted by the crackle of his radio. He answered it.

"Sheriff, this is Lyle. I'm at the newspaper office like you asked. I found something and I need to talk to you right away. In person. Something did happen in the woods of Blackthorn during the summer of 1975. Something that involved Randall Levert and your brother."

"Meet me at Blackthorn cottage," Dru said.

"You aren't going to believe this," Lyle said, excitement in his voice.

"At this point, I'm willing to believe anything. Randall Levert is dead in Blackthorn woods," Dru reported.

"You'd better find your brother then." Lyle's radio crackled. "Find him fast."

WATCHING THE PLAY of emotions on Dru's face, Rebecca found it difficult to contain her growing anxiety. Dru had never really given details about his brother except to say he was at Blackthorn, but it didn't take a detective to figure out there was a breach between them.

"I'll check on the horses," John said, and disappeared into the forest. Rebecca watched as Dru spoke to Jason, the deputy they were leaving behind. When he came back to her, she put a hand on his cheek and searched his eyes. "What are you thinking?"

"I'll tell you everything I know, but I want to tell John, too. He has a right to know this."

Rebecca linked her arm through his until the undergrowth made it impossible for them to walk side by side. When they got to the road, he motioned them all together.

"In the summer of 1975 something happened that changed Randall Levert's life dramatically," Dru said. "My brother changed, too. Lyle has found evidence that it happened here at Blackthorn. What if everything that's been going on here lately is aimed at preventing whatever happened in the past from coming out?"

"Sounds possible," John said, but there was still doubt in his voice. "But your brother would have been a boy then. What could a boy possibly have seen?"

"That's what I'm going to find out," Dru said. "All of these years Freddy's carried something around with him. Something awful. No one knew how to help him because no one knew what happened. Randall can't tell us now, but Freddy can. And if he doesn't, I'm afraid he's going to be the next target of the killer."

Rebecca swung into the saddle with some difficulty. She felt a sense of urgency. If what Dru said was true, they had little time to waste. If the killer was still at Blackthorn, perhaps he was in no hurry to leave because he hadn't finished what he'd set out to do.

"Go on," she said, waving the two men on. "Ride hard. I can't let Mariah run."

Dru hesitated.

"I have the cell phone you gave me," she said. "I'll be right behind you. I think Randall was trying to warn me last night—to make me leave Blackthorn for my own safety. If what you think is true, Freddy is the one in danger, not me."

"She's right," John said. "If your theory is correct, then Randall was acting as her friend."

"Go!" Rebecca ordered.

"I'll send someone back down the trail to walk with you," Dru said as Cogar wheeled, sensing the tension and eager for a run.

John took the lead on Diable with Dru at his heels. The horses, fit and energized, took off with a surge. Although it was hard to restrain Mariah, Rebecca forced the mare to maintain a walk. Her wound wasn't life-threatening, but such strenuous movement could aggravate the stitches.

Within a few minutes, the men were long gone and the peace and serenity of Blackthorn settled back over the trail. It was actually nice to have a few moments to think. A lot had happened in the past few days, and Rebecca felt as if it were all spinning around in her head. The rhythmic walk of the horse and the sounds of birds and small forest creatures was soothing, allowing her to slow down her thinking and try to piece things together in a way that made sense.

Dru's theory seemed more and more plausible as she thought about it. When Lottie Levert had been killed at Blackthorn, the underlying motive had been the buried treasure. But Aurelia and Marcus had discovered that and claimed it.

The only things of value here now were the artifacts being removed from the burial mound. But such items would require a very specialized knowledge to arrange a sale.

No, Rebecca decided, the artifacts weren't the motive, they were merely an end to a means. By taking the relics, someone was hoping to force the archaeological crew off the premises.

She was startled by another realization. The construction crew had valuable equipment on site, yet not a single act of sabotage had been directed against them. All of the focus was on the archaeological team.

Whoever was wreaking havoc at Blackthorn wasn't interested in what was being built. It was only what was being dug up. And if it wasn't the artifacts, what was it?

She thought back over all the things that had happened and still there seemed to be nothing to connect them. The puzzle would be snapped into place, she was sure of it. But at the moment, she couldn't make it fit. Once Dru spoke with his deputy and his brother, perhaps the missing pieces would fall into place.

Out of the corner of her eye she saw movement in the woods to her left. Mariah saw it, too. The mare snorted and edged to the opposite side of the lane.

Rebecca kept Mariah moving forward, holding her to a walk. Mariah wasn't a nervous animal, and her behavior made Rebecca tense. The mare sensed something.

She focused on the woods, but everything seemed still. More than likely it was a deer. The woods were full of them, their white tails bobbing as they leaped away. Up ahead, the road curved sharply. Ancient oaks grew in a line on either side, creating a canopy of graceful limbs. It was one of Rebecca's favorite parts of the estate, but she had an eerie sense that something waited there for her. Again Mariah started dancing.

"Easy, girl," Rebecca said. She was tempted to give the mare her head and let her run. It probably wouldn't be any more harmful than the way she was jigging up and down in the middle of the trail.

She was halfway through the tunnel of trees when a slight figure stepped out in the middle of the trail not ten yards ahead of her.

Rebecca felt her heart pound. Her legs tightened automatically on the horse and Mariah jumped forward, almost knocking into the stranger.

"Hey!" Regina Batson stepped out of the horse's way, putting a hand on Rebecca's leg as she bolted past. "Wait up a minute, Rebecca. Dru sent me to walk back with you."

"Did you see anyone else in the woods?" Rebecca asked, relieved to see Regina's familiar face.

Regina frowned. "I thought I heard something, but I assumed it was a deer. Let's get out of here, though, this place is beginning to creep me out."

More than glad to oblige, Rebecca nudged Mariah into a walk. The mare had settled down, and Rebecca took a long, deep breath. Her ribs ached from the tension, but she knew it wouldn't be long before they were healed.

"There's a shortcut to the barn from here," Regina said, pointing to a trail that was almost indiscernible. "Did Joey ever show it to you?"

"No," Rebecca said, surprised.

"He probably forgot about it. No one uses it. Brett showed it to me."

Rebecca wondered how Brett had come to be such a resident expert on the intricate trails of Blackthorn, but she didn't say anything, and followed Regina into the woods.

The trees grew closer and closer together, the limbs tangling among themselves. After being slapped in the face a half dozen times, Rebecca slid to the ground. It would be easier to walk in front of Mariah. The growth was less dense at ground level.

"Gosh, I'm sorry," Regina apologized. "Brett told me about this trail, but I never actually came down it. We should be at the barn in another ten minutes. It cuts off a lot of time and distance."

"Are you sure we're headed in the right direction?" Rebecca was busy protecting her eyes and Mariah's from the stinging limbs that slapped her face. But they were headed east instead of west.

"Oh, this is right. The trail twists and turns a little," Regina said. "We're going exactly where we need to go."

The brambles and underbrush crowded thicker and thicker until Rebecca wasn't certain there was even a trail. Regina was leading, and when she stopped, Rebecca followed suit. She was totally unprepared when a figure rose up from a clump of wild huckleberry bushes. She felt her arms pinned from behind, and though she struggled, she couldn't free herself from the firm grip. Her ribs were screaming with pain, handicapping her to the point that she found it pointless to fight. Someone grabbed Mariah's reins from her hands and pushed Rebecca toward Regina. It was the look on Regina's face that frightened Rebecca the most. She looked as if she'd won a prize.

DRU HANDED his brother a bottle of water and motioned for everyone else to leave.

"Lyle's going to be here any minute," Dru finally said. "He found something out about the summer of '75. Freddy, you have to tell me what happened. Randall Levert is dead."

Freddy lowered the water and gazed out at the river below them. They were sitting on one of the huge blocks that would soon be a part of the fast-growing house. The exterior walls were already well over twenty feet high. Dru couldn't help but observe that the house looked as if it had grown from the very bluff on which it stood. It was a work of architectural magic.

He focused on his brother. Freddy looked as if he'd been gut-punched. The color had drained from his face and he was staring at the river as though he'd never seen it.

"How did Randall die?" he finally asked.

"He was stabbed to death last night or this morning out in the woods."

"Christ, I told him to stay away from here. He was half-crazy about this place anyway."

"So you talked to him?" Dru asked.

"Who could avoid him? I'd walk out of my motel

room to get some ice and there he was, standing in the breezeway, waiting."

"What happened, Freddy? I'd rather hear it from you."

"I seriously doubt that, little brother. You're not going to want to hear what I have to say. It might tarnish your rose-colored view of the men in uniform that you hold so dear."

Dru felt the knot in his stomach tightening. Somehow he knew it would come back to this—to law enforcement and to their father. He could see so clearly now the changes that had occurred in Freddy, the way his older brother had grown to hate the men who represented the authority of the law.

"I need to know," Dru said. "Whatever it is, just tell me."

"You want to know about the summer of 1975? Well, like I said before, that was the summer Mom died. That was the summer Randall and I became good friends. He didn't have a dad, and his mother was so self-involved he might as well not have had one. Dad threw himself into being 'the best deputy' and then George Welsh didn't run for sheriff and Dad was elected. So it was like I didn't have a parent either. Randall and I had plenty of time to become good friends. And we did."

Dru sipped the water he'd gotten for himself. The day was going to be a scorcher, but it wouldn't compare to the searing words his brother spoke. For more than a quarter of a century Freddy had held all of this in. He'd paid a terrible price for it.

"Randall and I camped a lot up at Blackthorn. We hunted for the buried treasure. We had this idea that if we could find the treasure we could split it and then both of us would be able to…I don't know… I guess buy back our remaining parent's love."

Dru wanted to interrupt and tell Freddy that Stuart Colson had always loved him. Always. But he knew that words were ineffectual against the pain suffered by a neglected kid. "You saw something at Blackthorn, didn't you?"

"Yes," Freddy said. "We saw a woman burying the body of a baby. It was one of the most horrific things I've ever seen. She just dumped it in a hole and threw dirt on top of it. She could have been burying garbage for all of the concern she showed."

"No wonder Randall was obsessed with crying babies," Dru said. He felt sick. If someone had understood what was going on, Randall might have been helped before it was too late.

"Yeah. It hit Randall harder than me because he'd lost a little brother."

Dru wanted to close his eyes. He couldn't afford the luxury, though. The people of Natchez had failed Randall Levert and Freddy, too. "It must have been awful," Dru said. "You were just a kid. There was nothing you could do to stop it, but then you had it inside your head."

"We did try to stop it," Freddy said. His smile was cold, bitter.

"What do you mean?"

"We got on our bikes and we rode as hard as we could to the sheriff's office. All the way we were certain that evil woman would chase us down and kill us, too. In our minds she became a witch." Freddy tried for a smile and failed miserably. "We were just kids."

"Did you make it to the sheriff's office? Did you tell Dad?" Dru had to know the answer to this. All of his life he'd had a view of his father as a man who upheld the law, a man who had integrity and morals. Now that image was jeopardized. Freddy's answer could shatter Dru's entire past.

"We got to the sheriff's office. Dad was out. But Randall's uncle Lance Mullins was there. Remember, he was a deputy. We told him everything."

Freddy said the last with such finality that Dru didn't need to hear any more of it. He knew what had happened. "And he told you to shut up and keep quiet."

"He told us we had great imaginations. He told us that we were too old to be pulling pranks, that we could get in serious trouble for lying. And then he said that if we didn't want to get in really bad trouble, we should go home, stay away from Blackthorn, and keep our mouths shut."

"Did you try to tell Dad?" Dru asked.

"Yeah." Freddy looked back at the river. He fought the strong emotion that swept over him.

Dru wanted to go to him but he knew better. Freddy had fended for himself for too long to accept solace now.

"I told Dad. He even took a shovel and went up to

Blackthorn and dug where Freddy and I had seen her bury the baby. But it was gone. He thought I was lying. And I guess he told the deputy, because a week later, I was accused of stealing aftershave from Ratliff's Drug Store. Aftershave!" He made a derisive sound. "I was twelve years old."

"Lance Mullins told Dad he saw you take it and put it in your school bag," Dru said. He remembered the day clearly. Freddy's behavior and lying had almost broken Stuart Colson's heart.

"Deputy Mullins *said* he saw me. And then his best friend Elmo said I stole some BBs from the hardware store. And then it was that bicycle from Western Auto."

"Dad found the tire in the shed, Freddy. How did it—" Dru stopped. "Lance set the whole thing up. It was all done to discount your story about the dead baby."

"I was a twelve-year-old kid and every time I turned around, I was accused of stealing something or breaking something or doing something else. No one would believe me when I said I didn't do it."

"Dad thought you were just lying to protect yourself."

"But I wasn't."

"This would kill him." The words slipped out before Dru thought.

"Yeah, well I guess we're lucky he's already dead," Freddy said bitterly.

Dru swallowed the lump in his throat. There was no way to go back and change what had happened. Stuart

Colson had been a good man and a good sheriff, yet he'd failed his oldest son.

"Who was the woman with the baby?" Dru asked. "Did you recognize her?"

"That was the summer all those kids moved up here. You know, the commune. It was one of those girls, I suppose. We never really got a good look at her, and those kids took off after that. They were there one minute and then they were all packed up and gone the next."

"You didn't see the woman's face?"

Freddy shook his head. "All I remember is that she was crying. She was having a hard time with the shovel and all. And there was a car parked down the old driveway with a man in it. He was smoking cigarettes and the car was running."

"Do you remember where they buried the baby?"

"Sure, but there's no baby there. Dad looked, and then Randall and I went back and dug again ourselves. Someone moved that baby."

"It isn't too hard to guess who that was."

"Deputy Lance Mullins," Freddy said. " I heard he died of a heart attack about ten years ago."

"He did." Dru considered his next question. "If the girl was one of the hippies she could have been from anywhere. Do you suppose Lance was the father?"

"That would be a logical assumption," Freddy said, "but I don't have a clue. Randall was too afraid of his uncle even to talk about it. The things that happened were hard on me, but it was so much worse for Randall. He wouldn't leave the house. He had headaches all the time. He started clinging to his mother, and she didn't want him. Over the years I tried to make contact with him a few times but he'd never respond. I just dropped it. He had the car business and I thought maybe he'd finally put it all behind him. I thought it best to leave it all alone."

"Well, it's coming out now," Dru said. "It's like a big boil, festering all these years. Folks have been living on lies, but now it's all coming to a head."

"You sound like you're eager to see the past exposed," Freddy said, a frown on his face.

"I'm eager to get to the truth. Enough innocent people have been hurt. The only cure is the truth, Freddy. And I intend to see that it's told."

## CHAPTER EIGHTEEN

DRU STOOD UP when he saw John walking toward them. He felt annoyed at the interruption. He needed this time with his brother—time he'd been cheated out of because no one had taken the trouble to check into the story of two twelve-year-olds. Up to this point, Dru had shared everything with John, but he wasn't about to dole out portions of his brother's pain.

"Mariah came back to the barn. Riderless." John spoke with quiet urgency.

Dru felt his stomach drop. "I never should have left Rebecca to walk back alone." The full potential of what could be happening to Rebecca slammed into him.

Freddy got to his feet, shifting so they stood side by side. Dru glanced at his brother and their eyes connected. It had been a long time since they'd stood together.

"I thought she was perfectly safe, too," John said.

Dru's hand went instinctively to his side to check for the service revolver. His fingers moved to his cell phone. He quickly dialed the phone he'd given to Rebecca, but got the voice mail. "The phone has been turned off," he said.

"Mariah's been running. She's hot. Joey's walking her

cool, but she's okay. There was no sign of a struggle. At least no blood on the saddle," John told him.

Dru slipped the radio from his belt. Press answered immediately.

"Have you found anything?" Dru asked.

"Yeah, a dead end. Whoever we were following made it to one of the wider trails. They were picked up in a vehicle. I'd say some kind of four-wheeler based on the tracks. This was well planned out. We've been chasing our tails and I think someone wanted us to do exactly that."

The full meaning of Press's discouraged words weren't lost on Dru. They'd been set up, and whoever had killed Randall had help inside, from the Blackthorn crew. He looked at John and then at his brother. "Round up all of your men," he told John. "Contain the members of the archaeological crew. All of them. In one place where we can keep an eye on them. If Brett gives you any grief, do whatever you have to do to make him cooperative."

"What about the construction crew?" Freddy asked.

"I'll get Eugene to hold them," Dru said. "We need a head count and we need it right away, but I don't think our problem comes from there."

"What about me?" Freddy asked.

"Come with me. I'm going to need your help." Dru saw the flash of pride in Freddy's eyes and wondered how long he'd been waiting for such a moment.

They were just walking across the drive when Lyle

pulled up in a patrol car. He got out and glanced at Freddy. "Good morning, Freddy. It's been a lot of years," Lyle said. Dru saw there was a new respect in Lyle's eyes, and more than a few questions.

Without a word, Lyle handed Dru a photocopy of a newspaper page. Dru saw the story instantly. It was brief, but he recognized the school photos of Freddy and Randall. When no one else would listen to them, the two boys had gone to the newspaper with an account of what they'd seen.

The last paragraph was a disclaimer quoting Sheriff Stuart Colson, who said the boys' story had been investigated and nothing had been found. "It's been a hard summer for both of the boys, and they can't be blamed for trying to cook up an adventure." That was the sheriff's quote.

"It was true, wasn't it?" Lyle asked Freddy. "All along I wondered. But Lance said that Randall had broken down and admitted he was lying. After that, no one even thought about believing two kids. Especially not after one of them kept stealing and lying."

"Freddy never stole anything," Dru said quietly. "At least not at first. Not until everyone in town believed he was a thief."

Lyle whistled. "Well, I'll be. I see it now. Boy, your dad would be in a state. I can't tell you the hours he sat at his desk wondering how to help you, Freddy. He couldn't figure out how he'd let you down."

Dru expected his brother to pop off with something

smart. Instead Freddy swallowed. "Thanks, Lyle. It helps to know he was concerned."

"Concerned, hell. He was torn up. He would have given his right arm to change things for you. He just didn't know what else to do."

"Well, we're about to prove that Freddy wasn't lying back then," Dru said. "And I have a feeling that someone desperately wants to keep the truth buried here at Blackthorn."

REBECCA OPENED her eyes on a wave of pain and nausea. She was seated on the ground, her hands pulled behind her and tied around the trunk of a tree. She'd been left there almost half an hour before by Regina and the other person. Rebecca had never gotten a clear look at her, but she knew it was a woman.

Rebecca was through kicking herself for being so easily tricked. She'd moved on to trying to figure out what was happening. Somehow, Regina Batson was involved in everything that had been going on at Blackthorn. Rebecca wondered if Regina was acting at Brett's behest.

Lifting her head, she glanced around. There was no sign of Mariah or anyone else. She was alone. But Dru would find her. She held on to that and focused her mind on Regina Batson. Why would Regina do this? She was so young. So…ambitious. And so obviously smitten with Brett. There was no way to escape the logic that brought her back to Brett. But who was the other woman helping Regina? She realized she was about to find out.

Muffled by the woods, she heard two people talking. Arguing. She couldn't make out what they were saying. One was Regina. The other voice was lower, less easy to hear clearly.

Dropping her chin on her chest, Rebecca decided to feign unconsciousness. She might be able to pick up some valuable information if they thought she couldn't hear them.

ALL MEMBERS of the construction crew had been accounted for. Eugene Batson had been disgruntled at the delay, but Dru had convinced him to take his men into the shade for lunch. Several of John Ittawasa's men were unobtrusively watching over the construction workers. Now Dru stood with the archaeological team.

"We can't stand around all day waiting for you to think," Brett said caustically. "You can watch us just as easily as we dig."

"Shut up," Dru said. He was in no mood for Brett's haranguing.

"Either let us go hunt Rebecca or let us go back to work." Brett stepped closer. "If you'd been doing your job, she wouldn't be missing. Again."

There was clearly anger smoldering deep in Brett's eyes, and Dru wondered once again about his feelings for his boss. At times Brett seemed barely able to tolerate Rebecca. But it could be a cover-up for deeper emotions.

Dru glanced over the workers, most of whom were unperturbed by the delay. They'd gotten bottles of water and were sitting under the shade of a camp tent awning.

"Where's Regina?" Dru suddenly asked. Everyone was accounted for except her. At first he hadn't noticed because she wasn't really an official member of the team. She was a volunteer who came and went at her own discretion.

"I guess she went home," Brett said. "And a good thing, too. She was driving me nuts. Every time I turned around she was stuck to me like glue."

"You didn't seem to mind it so much," Dru said.

"It was cute at first, but it got a little old. She's spoiled rotten."

"Right," Winston said from his seat in the shade. "It got old about the time she started talking serious commitment." He laughed. "Brett started backpedaling like he was about to run off a cliff."

Brett threw Winston a dirty look. "You're just upset because she wouldn't go out with you."

"I understood. She's the kind of girl who aims for the top." Winston shrugged. "And I'd say she was a damn good shot. She had free run of the camp and came and went as she pleased. If she thought it was too hot to work, she didn't have to get sweaty."

"She was a volunteer," Brett defended himself. "She wasn't a paid employee. I couldn't make her work if she wanted to go home for a shower."

Dru listened to the exchange. A hunch was taking shape in his gut and he tried not to rush it. "When was the last time you saw Regina?" Dru asked.

"About two hours ago," Brett said. "She had a hair appointment or something. It's something she does every Monday." He rolled his eyes.

Dru nodded. "We'll check it out." He turned to walk away.

"What about us?" Brett asked.

Dru thought for a few seconds. "Go back to work, but no one leaves the burial mound. Stay up there. I'll have one of the deputies bring up something to eat in a little while."

"Okay, men, let's get back at it," Brett said, leading the way up the steps of the mound and back to the excavation.

"WHAT ARE WE going to do?" Regina asked, her voice rising with panic. "You said all we had to do was make them stop digging. You said—"

"I did this for you, Regina, so just shut up and let me think. We have to figure a way out of this."

Rebecca's impulse was to lift her head and look at Regina and the woman she could identify only by her voice—Millie Batson.

"You killed Randall," Regina said.

"Shut up! Don't you think I know it? It was an accident. I was trying to scare him. He was going to tell everything—he just flipped out. I thought if I could scare him, he'd shut up and go away. He tripped and fell on the knife. That's the God's honest truth."

"Fat chance anyone's going to believe that." Regina

walked over and stood by Rebecca. "And what are we going to do with her?"

"She's our ace in the hole."

"You mean *your* ace," Regina said. "I haven't hurt anyone, and I'll be damned if I'm going to go to jail for this. You're the one who smacked her with a tree limb. You're the one who stabbed Randall."

"Regina, I wouldn't let you take any blame for this," Millie said, her voice filled with sadness. "I did this so you wouldn't be smeared by my past. It was all for you."

"Why in the hell did you bury that baby here anyway?" Regina demanded.

"What was I going to do? Take it home and bury it in the garden?" Millie asked. "I was a kid. I was scared. And Lance Mullins was a married man. He told me if I didn't get rid of the body that he'd tell everyone in town I killed my own baby. I knew that I was considered nothing but trash, but I had one chance. Eugene had been coming up to the camp here, to talk to me. I knew he was interested, and I knew he was my one chance. So I took it the best way I knew how."

"Well, you've blown it now," Regina said in a nasty tone.

"The baby was born dead," Millie continued as if she hadn't heard her daughter. "I didn't kill her. I didn't do right by her, but I was just so afraid. I should have gotten a preacher or someone to say some words over her."

"Mama," Regina said, "snap out of it. We have to get

out of here. They'll be looking for Rebecca soon. We can either leave her here and let them find her, or we need to get her up and get moving."

"I wish I knew the right thing to do," Millie said, a great weariness in her voice. "I wish Randall had just kept out of this. When he came up on me in the woods last night, he scared me half to death. He told me he knew the truth. He said he knew someone had moved the baby to the Indian Mound, and he was going to tell. I only meant to frighten him. He fell onto the knife."

"No one's going to believe you," Regina said wearily. "You're going to jail for the rest of your life and all of this is going to ruin my future."

"No it won't, honey. I won't let it."

"What are you going to do?" Regina asked.

"Maybe I can disappear."

"And what about the baby's body you buried in the Indian Mound?" Regina asked.

"With Randall dead, no one will ever connect it to me," Millie said. "Randall and that Colson boy saw me bury the baby in the woods. It was Lance who moved it to the Indian mound. Not me. I doubt Freddy would even mention anything about a dead baby after the heat he took when he was a kid. Lance made it hard on him and on Randall, too."

"We have to stop the dig," Regina said. "I've done everything I can to keep them away from the grave. But they'll get there eventually." Regina sighed. "If you had only been able to frighten them away from the dig long enough for us to move the body."

Rebecca couldn't take it any longer. She lifted her head and looked at Millie and Regina. Millie was dressed all in black and her blond hair was tucked under a dark, short wig. "The only sensible thing to do is turn yourselves in."

"You would say that." Regina glared at Rebecca. "If you hadn't come here, none of this would have happened."

Rebecca had realized Regina was young and spoiled, but she hadn't realized how self-centered the young woman was. Regina saw only her own needs. It was both frightening and sad.

"Millie, if the baby died of natural causes, an autopsy can show that." Rebecca wasn't certain of this, but it sounded convincing. "And if Randall came up on you in the woods at night, it's very believable that he stumbled. This can all be explained."

"Can it?" Millie asked, a glimmer of hope in her eyes. "I never meant to hurt anyone. I just wanted to keep my secret. I didn't want Regina to suffer."

Rebecca wanted to say that she doubted Regina had the capacity to suffer for others, but she bit her tongue. She glanced at the young woman. "Did you ever care for Brett, or was that just a means to an end?"

"Let's just say that his arrogance is almost sublime." She rolled her eyes. "He needs an attitude adjustment."

And so do you, Rebecca thought. She could only wonder how Millie had gone so far astray in her love for her child.

She had three more questions for Millie. "You took the artifacts hoping that it would shut down the dig, didn't you?"

"I needed time to find the baby and move it," Millie said. "I've been hunting for the grave. I knew where I buried her, but Lance knew the boys had seen me. He moved the body and put it in the Indian mound. He told me if I ever tried to find it, he'd know, and he'd make me pay. I was afraid of him until he died. Lance had the power to hurt people like me. And he would have. After he died, so many years had passed and I was married to Eugene and had Regina to think about." Millie stared at the ground.

"Lance Mullins was the father?" Rebecca asked.

"It doesn't make a difference now if I tell," Millie said. "Yes, it was Lance. I was only seventeen, and he was married," she continued. "I was very naive. I'd never been with a man before, and he said he loved me. He promised to marry me. And I thought I loved him. But when I got pregnant, he didn't want me or the baby. He said he'd never loved me and that everyone in town would know I was just trash. He wanted me to have an abortion, but I didn't want that. He said if I didn't, he'd ruin me all over town. He said he'd fix it so no other man would even look at me. So I went up to Blackthorn to camp with the young people. There had been another baby born up there. I didn't know at the time the baby had died. There was just talk that girls could go up there and have their babies. I thought I could just give birth, like in the old days, and that me and my baby would live up there with the other young people and no one would bother us. But something went wrong. The cord was wrapped around the baby's neck. She didn't live but a few moments." She wiped a tear from her cheek.

"I'm sorry, Millie," Rebecca said. She looked at Millie and saw the careful makeup and the years of working hard to leave her past behind. But that had been impossible. The secret she'd had to drag behind her was just too big.

"I should have gone to the hospital. Maybe my baby would be alive today."

"And maybe not," Rebecca said. "Medicine wasn't as advanced then. That type of problem couldn't be prevented or changed." She had to give Millie what peace she could.

"Are we through trudging through the past?" Regina asked. "We have to decide what to do next."

"Where's Mariah?" Rebecca asked. She was worried about the horse.

"She pulled away from me and got loose," Millie said.

That could be either good or bad news. Mariah would go home and once she reached Blackthorn, there would be a general alert. "You know Dru will be looking for me," Rebecca said softly. "He'll be here soon."

"What are we going to do, Mother?" Regina demanded. "Think of something."

"Come back with me, give yourself up and return the artifacts," Rebecca said. "That's what you should do. I'll help you any way I can, and I'm sure Dru will, too."

Millie sighed and stood up. "I think she's right, Regina. That's the only thing to do. I can't run. I don't have money or a skill. And I'm tired of hiding all of this. I'm sorry."

"It's a little late to be sorry," Regina said. "If you give up, there'll be a trial. All of this will come out. I'll be a laughingstock in town."

Rebecca started to say something caustic but didn't. It would have been wasted breath. "Millie, you need to think about yourself and what's the best thing for you to do."

"I don't want Regina getting in trouble for taking the artifacts. She did it to help me." Millie glanced from Rebecca to her daughter. "I made her do it."

Rebecca nodded though she knew full well that Regina could never be made to do something against her will. What happened to Regina would be up to a judge. "You can tell all of this to Dru. He's a fair man."

"I don't know," Millie hesitated. "If I could get away, maybe—"

"Randall wasn't the only one who knew about the baby. Freddy Colson knew, too. And Freddy is at Blackthorn. He's on the construction crew. My guess is that he's tired of carrying the past, too. It's all going to come out, Millie, no matter what you do. You should help yourself."

"Untie her, please," Millie told her daughter. "It's time to face the music."

DRU POURED more wine into Rebecca's glass, then re-filled Freddy's and added just a little to Joey's. "To good friends," Dru said, lifting his glass, "and family."

"To the future," Freddy added. "I think it's going to be a very interesting one."

"To Mariah," Joey threw in.

Everyone took a sip of wine. Rebecca glanced around the table in the cottage where they'd all gathered. It had been two days since Millie had turned herself in. The body of her infant had been disinterred. A medical examiner would examine the remains and if no foul play was found, the baby would be buried in a cemetery.

Millie was free on a small bond pending a trial on the accidental death of Randall Levert. She was at home with Eugene, trying to work things out. Dru was still working with the prosecutor on the charges he would have to file against Regina. Rebecca could only hope, for Millie's sake, that it would be a misdemeanor rather than a felony and that intensive counseling would be part of her sentence.

"Have you spoken with the McNeeses?" Dru asked her.

"I finally got through to them in Spain. They almost decided to come home, but I convinced them we could handle everything."

"There was nothing they could do about Randall," Dru agreed.

"I should have kept in touch with him," Freddy said.

"The reason I came back to Natchez was to see him when I finally heard about what happened to his mother. But he wouldn't even talk to me. That one night, our lives changed. Randall had it even worse than me because Lance was his uncle, the only man he had to look up to. I think he would have given anything for Lance's respect. A kid doesn't understand that some men don't deserve to be loved that way."

"Randall's obsession with crying babies should have tipped me off," Dru said. "At first his mental deterioration was gradual. After his mother was killed, he went downhill quickly. At the end, though, he was trying to warn Rebecca. He used the things that were most terrifying to him—a baby in serious trouble. He was using those tapes really to try and frighten Rebecca out of danger."

"And when he paid me that visit," Rebecca said, "he was trying to help me."

"He wasn't trying to help when he hit me in the head," Joey said with a note of aggravation. "It hurt."

"That wasn't Randall," Dru said. "Regina admitted she did it. She didn't intend for you to fall from the barn. That was an accident. She intended to start a small fire in the barn in the hopes that she could make you leave Blackthorn. You were a real thorn in her side, Joey. You kept showing up and interfering in her mischief, which is why she was always complaining about you to Brett. That's why he also griped about you. Regina couldn't be sure where you'd turn up, and it was cramping her ability to steal the artifacts."

"She could have killed the horses with a fire." Joey wasn't about to forgive her for that.

"She could have, but you prevented it," Dru said, patting his arm.

"I don't like her," Joey said. "She stole things."

"I don't like her either," Rebecca said, "but at least she's returned the artifacts she took. Now John has the Black Stick, the bowl and a dozen other artifacts in his care. Brett's been very busy."

"And still mean," Joey said. "He yelled at me this morning."

Rebecca couldn't hide her smile. Some things never changed. Brett was as surly as ever. More so since his crew had been teasing him about Regina's motives.

"I'm hearing some very interesting facts about the Mound Builders," Freddy said. "The relics Brett is finding mean a lot to the Indians." He paused. "John has offered me a job in Philadelphia, Mississippi. They're developing a resort for the Choctaw people. He wants me to be in charge of some of the construction."

"Are you going to take it?" Dru asked, not bothering to disguise the hope in his voice.

"Yes, I am."

"Good." Dru's smile widened. "You'll be close enough so I can see a lot of you. And you'll be able to do me a big favor."

"What's that?" Freddy asked.

"Serve as best man in my wedding."

There was a moment of surprise before Joey stood up and yelled. "Another Blackthorn wedding? We can have it in the garden. In the fall, when all of my lilies are blooming."

Rebecca looked at Dru and saw his answer in his eyes. "Fall would be lovely, Joey," she said.

"My little brother doesn't waste any time, does he?" Freddy asked, lifting an eyebrow. "Are you sure about this, Rebecca? After all, he comes from a family with a checkered past."

"It's not his past I'm interested in," Rebecca said sotto voce. "In fact, I've seen how much damage the past can do. Maybe we should all pretend that we've forgotten our past. We could live only for the moment."

"There are things about the past I don't want to forget," Dru said, giving Rebecca a look that made everyone laugh.

"Too bad," Rebecca said with a mock sigh. "You can live on your past memories. I intend to create new ones!"

Dru stood up and pulled her into his arms. "In that case, maybe our company should leave," he said.

"I'm going to the garden," Joey said, taking the hint. "Freddy, come help me decide where to plant the spider lilies."

"You're on, buddy," Freddy said. They slammed the cottage door behind them as they left.

Rebecca turned her face up to Dru with a smile. "That was rather rude of us, don't you think?"

"I've already forgotten what happened. I'm only focused on this very second. And your wonderful lips. And all of the places I'm going to kiss you." He grinned. "Unless, of course, you'd rather talk about the wedding."

"No, I like your original plan just fine. Stop talking. And start kissing."

\* \* \* \* \*

*Fall in Love with...*

# MEN
# *in* UNIFORM

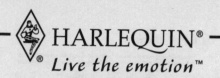

# SPECIAL EDITION™

**Emotional, compelling stories that capture the intensity of living, loving and creating a family in today's world.**

Special Edition features bestselling authors such as Susan Mallery, Sherryl Woods, Christine Rimmer, Joan Elliott Pickart— and many more!

For a romantic, complex and emotional read, choose Silhouette Special Edition.

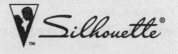

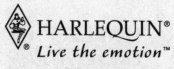

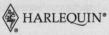

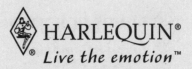

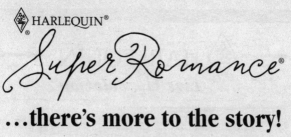
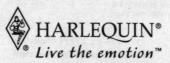

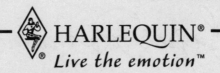

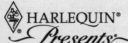